"So, if I wanted a tour guide, you'd be the one to hire, right?"

Jack watched Kat carefully for her response.

"I've never done that before."

"Would you be interested?"

"Do you mean I'd drive you around in my car?"

Jack shook his head. "On my bike. You could give me a running history of the area and tell me where to go."

Kat frowned slightly as if thinking over the proposition. "When?"

"Tomorrow? If it doesn't rain."

"Well, I don't have my kids tomorrow...so I suppose I could. But I couldn't do it free."

"Of course not." He did some quick math. Eight hours. Forty dollars an hour seemed fair. He quoted her the price.

"Seriously? Deal." She flashed a bright smile then continued with what she'd been doing.

He wasn't _____ _____ ut in two days he'd _____ es. So far, he wa _____ He only hoped th

After all, there had to be worse things than riding around the mountains with a beautiful blonde on the back of his motorcycle.

Dear Reader,

If you're a first-time visitor to Sentinel Pass, welcome! If you've read the first two books in this series, *Baby by Contract* and *His Brother's Secret,* and are dying to find out which member of the Wine, Women and Word Book Club gets to tell her story next, I won't keep you waiting. It's Kat.

Katherine Petroski may be a two-time loser at marriage, but she's a firm believer in the power of swoo...I mean *love.* After all, she has two amazing kids to show for her mistakes. Her only regret is not loving their fathers enough to stay married. She's not going to make that mistake again. Even when she accidentally sleeps with a handsome biker who turns out to be an orthodontist from Denver.

Jackson Treadwell is determined to prove he's not a stuck-in-a-rut prude with no sense of adventure. He buys a Hog, takes a leave of absence from his practice and heads for the hills...the Black Hills. His first night in Deadwood he manages to scratch "instigate a bar fight" off his to-do list. And although he doesn't realize it at the time, he also crosses off "meet the girl of my dreams." Literally.

I must thank my brother-in-law, David Salonen, and his amazingly tolerant wife, Karryn, for bringing to my attention the power of "swoo." Karryn, I'm glad you ducked too late. Dave, long may the Swoo be with you. And thanks also to Dave Meek and Tom Salonen for giving me an inside glimpse at the Sturgis Bike Rally.

For up-to-the-minute insider information on what's happening in Sentinel Pass, a Black Hills photojournal and contest opportunities, please visit my Web site, www.debrasalonen.com. Or write me at P.O. Box 322, Cathey's Valley, CA 95306.

Happy reading,

Debra Salonen

DADDY BY SURPRISE
Debra Salonen

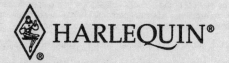

TORONTO • NEW YORK • LONDON
AMSTERDAM • PARIS • SYDNEY • HAMBURG
STOCKHOLM • ATHENS • TOKYO • MILAN • MADRID
PRAGUE • WARSAW • BUDAPEST • AUCKLAND

Recycling programs
for this product may
not exist in your area.

ISBN-13: 978-0-373-71540-4
ISBN-10:   0-373-71540-4

DADDY BY SURPRISE

www.eHarlequin.com

Printed in U.S.A.

ABOUT THE AUTHOR

Debra comes from a long line of storytellers. At slumber parties, her mother would enthrall Deb's girlfriends with stories of growing up on the prairie near Pierre, South Dakota. (For you *Jeopardy* purists, that's pronounced Peer.) One goose-bump-inducing story involved unearthing a casket of a pioneer woman in an unmarked grave. Deb had no problem picturing her mother sitting in the dark, guarding the poor woman's remains while Grandpa Bagby rode back to town for the sheriff. It was a better story than the one involving rattlesnakes…. Nobody got any sleep on the nights she told *that* story.

Books by Debra Salonen

HARLEQUIN SUPERROMANCE

1098—MY HUSBAND, MY BABIES
1104—WITHOUT A PAST
1110—THE COMEBACK GIRL
1196—A COWBOY SUMMER
1238—CALEB'S CHRISTMAS WISH
1279—HIS REAL FATHER
1386—A BABY ON THE WAY
1392—WHO NEEDS CUPID?
    "The Max Factor"
1434—LOVE, BY GEORGE
1452—BETTING ON SANTA*
1492—BABY BY CONTRACT**
1516—HIS BROTHER'S SECRET**

SIGNATURE SELECT SAGA

BETTING ON GRACE

HARLEQUIN AMERICAN ROMANCE

1114—ONE DADDY TOO MANY
1126—BRINGING BABY HOME
1139—THE QUIET CHILD

*Texas Hold 'Em
**Spotlight on Sentinel Pass

To Wanda Ottewell,
for listening to my characters with such an open mind,
and for providing a safe environment for risk-taking.

CHAPTER ONE

KAT PETROSKI patted the bulge in her front jeans pocket. Not bad for a Wednesday, but nothing compared to what the regular servers would make that weekend when the town of Deadwood, South Dakota, filled with people celebrating the Days of '76—a yearly commemoration of the gold rush–era town's founding. For a week every July, thousands of people came to the Black Hills to see the rodeo, show off their Harleys and drink gallons of beer at Pop's, the popular Main Street saloon where she was filling in for a friend.

"Never count your tips before last call," Becky Jennings, her mentor in the bartending/waitress business, had once told her. A flat night of tips could make the time seem endless.

Bec, who decided she needed another day at home recovering from gallstone surgery, was a hard-drinking, chain-smoking, fortysomething gal who took no crap from anyone. Kat often wished she could be more like her, but she didn't have the height, weight or metabolism for it. A couple of beers was usually enough to put Kat under the table, which was why she didn't drink.

She'd made that mistake twice in the past and had two unplanned but gorgeous mistakes to show for it. Her

sons, Tag and Jordie. The true loves of her life. At the
time of their conceptions, she'd have given that title to
their fathers, but neither Pete Linden nor Drew Petroski
had lived up to their promises. They'd married her—
once her father mentioned the word *shotgun*—but
neither marriage had lasted. For reasons she was beginning to think might be linked partly to her parents'
divorce when she was six.

Jordie's age, she thought with a sigh. Jorden Petroski.
The sweetest, most eager-to-please kid on the planet—
just like she'd always been. Eight-year-old Tag, on the
other hand, was tough. Because he had to be. That was
her fault, too.

"Hey, Kat, I need another beer," a voice boomed
from a table in her section. "And give this guy a shot of
Jäger. He's a virgin."

The man doing the ordering was Brian Whitlock. A
regular. He drove a rig for Black Hills Moving and
Trucking. About ten years older than her thirty-one, he
lived near Nemo with his wife and three little kids. But
he spent the better part of his life—and most of each
paycheck—in one of the many bars and casinos along
Deadwood's main street. The person he was ordering a
shot for was a stranger. Clearly a R.U.B., an acronym
that stood for rich, urban biker.

In this case, the man fit the name completely. His
leather chaps were too pristine to be more than a week
or two old. His expensive lace-up boots showed dust but
no real scuffs. A hint of silver was evident in the side-
burns showing beneath his do-rag, which was black
with orange skulls on it.

When he'd first walked into the bar, she'd given him

a quick assessment—an acquired skill and necessary survival tactic in this business. Mid-thirties. No wedding band. She put his height at six feet, weight in the 180 range. Maybe less. The pecs and biceps displayed by his spanking-new black T-shirt told her he wasn't a weight-lifter. There was clear definition and form, but no look-at-me bulk. The logo on his shirt told her he knew how to use the Internet because she'd ordered one just like it for her stepbrother. Those shirts wouldn't be available locally for another week and a half, when the 2008 Sturgis Bike Rally started.

Like Deadwood's Days of '76, the rally drew all kinds of people from all over the world. The bikers brought their own brand of craziness, but their money was a boon for the Hills' economy. Quite a few came early and stayed for both events.

"Coming right up."

She slipped behind the made-to-look-antique bar, since Guy, the bartender, was playing dice with a couple of regulars while waiting for the night to pick up. Guy was a decent fellow, retired from some branch of the armed forces and big enough to keep order when things got rowdy. He acknowledged her with a nod as she filled the shot glass.

She inhaled a lungful of smoke-tainted air as she headed across the room. She wasn't surprised to see the R.U.B. watching her—she'd chosen to wear her Victoria's Secret push-up bra and low-cut tank top for a reason.

As Pete—ex-hubby number one—so eloquently put it when she'd unloaded Tag and his camping gear at his father's house in Rapid City, "I see you're wear-ing your Tits for Tips outfit. Ya should've gotten that boob job when I offered. Then you'd really haul in the cash."

Pete prided himself on being a breast man. Why he'd dated her was still a mystery—given the fact she was a modest B-cup. She'd turned down his offer of breast enhancement because she was still nursing his son at the time he offered. By the time Tag was done nursing, Pete had found himself a new, more generously endowed woman. Apparently a divorce was cheaper than surgery.

Pete was taking Tag and Tag's half brother, Aiden, camping at Deerfield Lake until Sunday, but he'd called that morning to say he was running late and needed Kat to deliver Tag, instead of his picking up their son on the way to the lake as planned. This meant Kat had had to dress for work earlier than she would have preferred, drive to Rapid, drop off her son, then take the I-90 to Sturgis to straighten out the mess regarding her vendor-booth application—which she'd just learned had somehow gotten lost—before heading to Deadwood. More driving, more gas.

Kat's other son, Jordie, had left earlier that morning to attend a Native-American powwow with Char, her good friend and fellow member of the Wine, Women and Words book club. Unlike Pete, Char had picked up Jordie. Right on schedule.

"Here you go, gentlemen," she said, carefully setting down the glasses within their line of vision but not so they could be knocked over too easily. Both patrons appeared to be about halfway down the road to drunk.

The R.U.B.'s gaze moved from her chest to her face. His eyes, which were an interesting shade of gray, seemed a bit out of focus, but he blinked twice and smiled. "Thangs."

The *K* didn't come out right, but his voice was pleasant—deep and cultured. And his smile was almost as sweet as Jordie's, only this guy's teeth were toothpaste-commercial white and beautifully aligned. It was a little early to tell, but she was afraid Jordie's were going to turn out as crowded and misaligned as Tag's. She and Pete argued about the inevitability and cost of orthodontia nearly every time they saw each other.

"I'm not really one, you know. A vershin," he said. "Eggcept where this stuff is concerned." He brought the glass to his nose and sniffed. "Urgh." He paused a moment as if debating whether or not to drink it, then he let out a sigh. *"Ifnotnowwhen?"* He ran the words together, then downed the drink in one gulp.

When he looked at her, his pretty gray eyes twinkled. She tried to convince herself it was the booze making them water, but then he winked. Maybe he wasn't as drunk—or as much of a R.U.B.—as she first thought.

That was when it struck her that he was actually rather handsome. A second later a cannon-fire warning sounded in her head. *Swoo alert. Duck, lady, duck.*

The last was an inside joke only her friend Libby would have gotten, but Lib understood better than anyone the power of *swoo*—a made-up word Kat's mother had used to explain why the women in Kat's family were drawn to downright awful choices in men.

"Some people might call it charisma, but that's a little fancy for the spell certain men can cast over us. Might be we're genetically susceptible to faulty pheromones," her mother had theorized—too late to do Kat any good.

By the time Kat understood the power swoo had on her, she was pregnant a second time and saying "I do" with Drew Petroski—the cutest, most immature outfielder she'd ever had the misfortune to play softball with.

She shifted sideways and leaned down to pick up the man's empty glass. She noticed his gaze followed the lace that peeked above the dip in her neckline. "That's nine seventy-five," she told them. "The beers are half price because of happy hour."

She braced herself for a ten and a "keep the change" from Brian, but to her surprise the stranger fished a twenty from the hip pocket of his new-looking jeans and dropped it on her tray. "The rest is yours," he said, his words overly correct, as though he was trying to act sober for her benefit. "For providing yet another rule-breaking, risk-taking, fantasy-living step toward reinventing myself. Y'know what I mean?"

Not even close. "Sure. Thanks." She had no idea what that speech was all about, but he wasn't the first drunk to think he'd found the road to enlightenment through an alcohol-induced haze. "Another round?" she murmured, backing away so fast she bumped into two people making their way toward the door.

"Oops," she said. "Sorry."

A man and a woman. Both in leathers—broken in in a way the R.U.B.'s weren't. The man—a big, burly guy with thick, fat fingers sticking out of black leather demi-gloves—steadied Kat with both hands, acknowledging her apology with a low grunt. The woman apparently thought her man's sweaty, unpleasant touch lingered a millisecond too long, because she shoved Kat back toward the table she'd been serving with a powerful straight-arm.

"Back off, bitch," she snarled, her bloodshot eyes squinting lethally.

Kat managed to keep her balance, but her hip grazed the back of the chair occupied by the big tipper. "Sorry," she told him.

"Don't apologize to that pretty-boy biker wannabe," the woman growled. Her voice held the same two-pack-a-day roughness Kat's mom's had held—before her diagnosis of throat cancer. She didn't smoke anymore, but she didn't talk much, either, thanks to the valve in her windpipe.

The woman, who was only a few inches taller than Kat, but a good hundred pounds heavier, took a breath, making her ponderous breasts strain against the American-flag tank top. "God, I'm sick of all these weekend warriors showing up thinking they're cool because they can afford to buy a Hog off the showroom floor," she said in disgust. "It's even worse at the rally. That's why Buster and me came early."

Buster, who was bald beneath the black scarf tied tight to his large, square head, looked slightly embarrassed. "Let's go, Mo."

As in one of the Three Stooges? Kat thought. No. Too fat for Moe.

"Mo? Are you sure? She looks more like Curly," someone said, voicing Kat's thought.

Kat covered her lips with her free hand to keep from laughing. Any response on her part would only add fuel to the fire. She just hoped the heavyset woman in question hadn't heard—

"Why you smart-ass, little shit. I was riding bikes when you were still sucking teat. What are you? A lawyer? Tax accountant? Some kind of desk jockey, I know that much."

The man turned sideways to the table so he could see the woman more clearly. He started to stand, but Kat put her hand on his shoulder and pressed downward. This tiff was on the verge of becoming a fight, and no one came out ahead when that happened.

"Oh, come on, folks," Kat said, keeping her voice light. "Let's not go there. Name calling doesn't make anyone feel better. Mo, right? Short for Maureen? I have an aunt Maureen."

"Who the f—"

"Hey. Watch your language. There's a lady present."

The words were so outdated, Kat had to laugh. "Listen, John Wayne, thanks for standing up for me, but I hear that word about nine thousand times a night."

"Are you sayin' I ain't a lady?" Mo asked. Her fists, each of which easily made two of Kat's, started bouncing around her sides. She gestured behind her for backup and nearly popped Kat by accident.

Kat dodged the blow, then had to scramble to keep from getting mowed over by the guy she'd been protecting from a pummeling. "Listen, you obnoxious cow, you can't just throw your considerable weight around and threaten hardworking barmaids who are trying to keep the peace. You're a disgrace to that flag, which, by the way, was never meant to be worn as bra. Half the stars are—"

Whatever slight he'd intended was stopped by a set of leather-encased knuckles that glanced off his elegant cheekbone. Kat had witnessed enough bar fights to know that if the giant biker had been sober, the punch would have broken the R.U.B.'s nose and maybe a couple of teeth. As it was, the impact sent the unsuspecting fellow straight into Kat's arms.

Her serving tray, which she'd tucked under her arm, hit the floor with a loud bang. Mo gave them all one last sneer, then grabbed Buster's meaty arm and split. Seconds later, the roar of a Harley outside shook the windows.

The sound made the man, who had Kat partially pinned against the table, lift his head. "Are they gone?"

In a heartbeat, she realized two things: his anatomy fit hers almost perfectly and his was the sneaky kind of swoo—you didn't know how powerful it was until you were leveled by it.

With a harrumph of disgust—at herself, not him—she pushed him back. "What kind of idiot picks a fight with drunken bozos three times his size?"

"Were they really that big?" he asked, gingerly rubbing his jaw. "I left my glasses in my motel room."

She looked at Brian, who let out a raucous hoot, then yelled something about the size of the stranger's *cojones*.

Kat shook her head in disgust. "Do you need an ice pack for that?"

"I don't think anything is broken."

"Well, the night is young. Sit down. I'll get you some ice, anyway."

She was gone before Jack could tell her not to bother. He was staying just up the street and was pretty sure he could walk back to his motel without help. Not that he didn't appreciate the concern he'd read in her pretty blue eyes, but this was his first bar fight.

One more thing to cross off the list, he thought, trying not to smirk. Smirking hurt. He might even wind up with a black eye. If he did, he'd use his digital camera and e-mail a shot of it to Jaydene, his ex-fiancée. Petty, sure, but a part of him wanted to show her proof that he, Jackson Boyd Treadwell III, wasn't a stuck-in-a-rut orthodontist with no sense of adventure. He could walk on the wild side when he wanted to. He'd simply been too busy going to school, then establishing his practice, to have time to experience any such recklessness.

Not that getting punched out actually had been on his list of things to do when he came to the Black Hills, but there'd been a moment when he stood up to that female bully that he'd felt heroic—invincible. Until her trained gorilla decked him. Luckily, the cute little barmaid whose honor he'd been defending was there to cushion his fall. In a really nice way.

He didn't usually find himself attracted to petite women. His mother was short, but he doubted if anyone had ever called her petite. Rosaline Treadwell was a five-foot-two-inch dynamo who had only recently traded in her stiletto heels for golf shoes when she retired from the bank where she was a vice president in charge of corporate loans. She'd been instrumental in helping Jack buy the building that housed Treadwell and Associates. "It's never too late for a perfect smile" was his marketing slogan, since his group of three dentists—two other orthodontists and one endodontist—catered to all ages. Jack specialized in adults. Kids were not his cup of Kool-Aid, as his sister liked to say.

"Hey, man," Brian, the guy who had offered to buy him a drink—which Jack had ended up paying for—said. "You got off lucky. I know that Buster dude. I seen him knock a guy unconscious once over in Sturgis. You could be missing some teeth."

Jack squeezed his jaw experimentally and bit down. Nothing loose. Thank God. He'd never hear the end of it from his mother if he returned to Denver needing emergency dental work. "Yeah, lucky me," he muttered.

"Here you go," the waitress said, returning with a glass of ice in one hand and a thick wad of paper towels in the other. She set both items in front of him. "The bar rags all smelled funky and I couldn't find a zipper kind of baggie. That's what I use when my kids get hurt. I put a couple of cubes in the bag, then cover it with a towel and let them whack the ice with a hammer. Distracts them from the pain and gets rid of some of their frustration."

He could picture the image perfectly. He would have smiled, but his face was beginning to ache. "You have kids? Plural?"

Maybe he was drunker than he thought because he could see his harmless question had caused some offense. Her pretty blue eyes narrowed. "Yes, I do. Two boys."

"I...um...meant that as a compliment. You look too young to have one kid, let alone two."

Some of the fight went out of her posture. "Oh. Thanks. Let me buy you another shot," she said, turning on the heel of her thick-soled running shoes. She paused to pick up the tray she'd dropped, then hurried across the room.

Her trim build reminded him of a long-distance runner—compact and lean. He swam laps every morning, but he'd been thinking about diversifying his workout routine to see more than two walls at opposite ends of his pool.

When she returned, he asked, "Do you run?"

She looked at Brian as if the question required an interpreter.

"10 Ks? Marathons?" Jack tried.

"Me?" Her eyes sparkled with humor, but there was something sad in her expression, too. As if the word triggered a case of might-have-beens. "I run after my kids. That's about it."

"Weren't you in track in high school, Kat?" Brian asked. "I swear, that's what somebody told me. Because you were always the fastest on our softball team."

She shrugged. "Another lifetime, Brian. Or maybe a dream. I can't remember which." She leaned closer to Brian and added something Jack couldn't quite catch.

Jack hated being the odd man out. People whispering behind his back. He'd experienced enough of that when rumors about his father had pretty much ruined his chance to fit in and have a normal life.

He dumped the glass of ice upside down on the towels. A couple of cubes rolled off the edge of the scarred tabletop.

She squatted to retrieve them, which gave Jack a fine view of her bosom—fleshy tan mounds squashed together by a black lace bra that peeked ever so provocatively above the edge of her low-cut top.

He forced himself to look away. Why? He asked himself as he slapped one corner of the paper towel over the other. She'd dressed provocatively to draw attention. Only an uptight prude—as Jaydene had labeled him—would be too self-conscious to stare.

Before he could change his mind and take another look, she bounced to her feet, dropping the dirty cubes into Brian's empty beer glass. She picked it up, then said, "I didn't mean to be rude, but anybody who knows me knows I don't have time to work out. I love sports, but I haven't even played softball since the year Brian and I were on the same team."

"That's 'cause she got knocked up a second time," Brian said gauchely, causing twin spots of red to appear on her cheeks.

Jack palmed the already soggy handful of ice and paper towel like a wad of dog poop from one of Jaydene's whippets and pressed it against his cheek. His whole face was starting to hurt.

"Do you have any aspirin or acetaminophen on you?" she asked, her brow knit in concern.

He shook his head.

She glanced over her shoulder toward the bar. "I'll bring you something. I'm a mom. I don't leave home without a full pharmacy in my purse. But you have to be discreet, okay? My boss thinks he could get sued if you had a bad reaction."

"I'm not allergic to anything," Jack said, trying not to move his jaw too much. His words probably sounded garbled, but she smiled as if she understood him completely.

Like that was possible. No woman he'd ever met really got him—including his fiancée and his mother. Everyone saw the outward signs of success—nice home, luxury car, booming practice—and assumed he was someone he wasn't. Happy, secure, confident. All things he pretended to be.

It had taken a surprise and rather shocking confrontation with the woman he'd intended to marry to make him question his everyday reality. Like him, Jaydene pretended to be someone she wasn't. Serious—she worked in a bank and volunteered at an adult school. Responsible—four years older than Jack, she seemed wise, witty and slightly irreverent. And in the three-plus years they'd been dating she'd never once expressed an interest in kinky, multiple-partner sex until the afternoon he showed up unexpectedly at her home and found her involved in a ménàge a trois—via the Internet.

Just picturing the lurid image of her legs spread on either side of her laptop with the little eyeball camera trained on her most private parts as her two partners—both men—did the same was almost enough to make him toss his last shot of anis-flavored booze.

After the initial shock had worn off, they'd talked. She'd called him repressed. Unadventurous. Boring. She'd implied that her participation in online sexual encounters was because she knew he would have shot down any suggestion that, as a couple, they try swinging.

And she was right.

He'd swung in a different direction. He took a long overdue vacation from work. Kissed his mom and sister goodbye, then jumped on his shiny new Harley and headed to the Black Hills. Close enough to Denver to get back quickly if he was needed, yet far enough away that it wasn't home.

He'd picked the Black Hills of western South Dakota for two reasons. First, he was a closet fanatic of all things Old West. He didn't decorate his house in antiques or anything, but he watched every television series and miniseries that came along. Every incarnation of *Lonesome Dove*. He had the entire *Deadwood* series on DVD. He also owned an extensive collection of western movies, from *Dances with Wolves* to the John Wayne classics. Recently he'd turned to romance novels to get his western fix, since his two favorite novelists, Zane Grey and Louis L'Amour, were long dead.

Second, the Hills had a reputation that almost rivaled Las Vegas's infamous "What happens in Vegas stays in Vegas" slogan. He was ready to cut loose and experience what Jaydene claimed he'd been missing. This was his time and he planned to live it to the fullest.

She just hadn't warned that the experience would hurt.

CHAPTER TWO

KAT WAITED PATIENTLY for the R.U.B. to leave. She'd brought him a glass of water about an hour ago without his asking, but he'd failed to take the hint. Or stop drinking. Now he claimed to be killing the pain, but she had a feeling he wasn't talking about the ache in his bruised jaw. Her gut told her this guy had woman problems.

"Kat!" Brian hollered, motioning her over. "Jack here says he wants to get a tattoo. I told him that was Master Jäger talking, but he says he don't know anybody by that name."

Laughing at his own joke, Brian would have toppled off his chair if Kat hadn't been close enough to steady him. "Can I call your wife to come pick you up, Brian? You're in no condition to drive."

"Huh? No. Me'n my friend need another round."

"Not unless your friend plans on letting you sleep it off in his hotel room." Brian wasn't a bad guy; he just didn't know his limit.

"Aw, Kat, you're no fun. What happened to you? You used to be fun. 'Member when we played on the same softball team? You 'n me 'n…um, what was your second husband's name? I forgot."

She rolled her eyes. "Me, too. About as often as he

forgets to send his child support." She didn't care if that was more information than the stranger who was staring at her needed to know. She looked at him and said, "What about it, mister? Are you claiming responsibility for this inebriated galoot?"

His left eyebrow rose in a perfect arch that gave his face a sort of Daniel Craig look. She'd seen that particular James Bond movie three times. Now, there was a man with big-screen swoo. "How 'bout if I buy him dinner?"

"Good idea. Make sure he orders coffee, not wine."

He nodded but made no effort to get up. She assumed he was waiting for a menu, so she explained, "We're just a bar, but there are a bunch of restaurants around. The one next door has a pretty decent chicken-fried steak."

He blanched, which made the faint bruise on his cheek more noticeable.

"Are you feeling sick?"

He shook his head. "No. It's just…well, my dad took drugs for his high cholesterol since his mid-forties, had quadruple bypass surgery and suffered a fatal heart attack when he was fifty-eight. A chicken-fried steak sounds lethal." He paused a moment, then shrugged. "That's what I'm going to order."

"You have a death wish?"

"Me? Heck, no. Ask anybody who knows me. I'm boringly predictable. Especially where food is concerned. I wash my prewashed spinach," he said, tellingly.

She didn't see what was so bad about that. She might, too, if she could afford the bagged stuff.

"This trip is about doing things I would never normally do," he added.

"Like get a tattoo," Brian repeated. "That's why he

came in here. To get drunk enough not to feel the needles, but I told him how bad it was when I got this baby done." He yanked up his shirtsleeve to show them the large, colorful parrot on his upper arm. "Hurt like freakin' hell. Worth it, though. I call her Linda, after my wife. That's Spanish for beautiful."

"Leen-da," Kat said softly, using the accent she'd picked up while satisfying her foreign-language minor.

The stranger must have heard because he looked at her sharply...until Brian slapped his hand on the table. "Hey. I know. You can hire Kat to do your tat, man. She don't use needles. She does that other stuff. What's it called, Kat?"

"Henna," she supplied, wishing the bar was busier so she'd have an excuse to get out of this conversation. She'd operated a booth for years at summer street fairs, giving artful, semipermanent tattoos. Henna was a stain that bonded to the skin and didn't wash off, but faded slowly enough to create the illusion of a tattoo—without the regret that often came later.

Brian's newfound friend looked interested. "That's brownish red, isn't it? But you can do black, right? A friend of mine got a really elaborate armband design that looked like the real thing from a distance. And in photos," he added, as though that was important to him.

She assumed he was one of those people who put a lot of stock in what others thought. The kind who'd judged her all her life.

"I only do henna."

He scrutinized her a moment. "You don't have any black henna?"

"Actually, there's no such thing. Black dye contains

PPD. I can't remember what that stands for, exactly, but it's outlawed by the FDA."

He exchanged a look with Brian. A guy look. She knew it well. *Law? Law? We don't need no stinkin' laws.* It was the same with marriage vows. "But it's still used," the man insisted. "Like I said, my friend was on a beach in Florida over spring break when he had it done. No side effects. No problems whatsoever."

"Yeah. Same with my wife," Brian said. "Linda had one done on her leg when we were in Mexico. Liked it so much she bought a kit. She was going to give Kat some competition at the street fair but never got around to it. Like usual. It's collecting dust with all the other crap in my garage."

"Could I buy it?" the R.U.B. asked.

"Hell, you can have it, man. No problem."

Kat had an opinion about Brian's wife's lack of successful endeavors, but she kept it to herself. "How long ago did you buy it?" she asked. "An out-of-date product could be even more dangerous."

Brian frowned in thought, but before he could come up with a date, her prospective customer said, "I'm healthy as a horse, and like I said earlier, not allergic to anything. Will you do a design in black if I supply my own ink?"

"Don't you want to know how much I charge?"

"Not really," he said, confirming her first impression. He must have money. And she'd be a fool not to let a hundred bucks or so float into her pocket—even if she wasn't crazy about using a product she'd never tried.

He had several plusses in his favor. He wasn't a sweaty, stinky behemoth, like several of her former clients. And a part of her was really curious about what was under that do-rag. A receding hairline, no doubt.

"You don't have to worry about the price, Jack," Brian said, slapping the man on the back. "Kat'll treat you fair. She's gonna be a schoolteacher pretty soon and then she won't have to work here no more."

Kat grasped the convoluted logic. She'd been working at a bar too long. She was beginning to talk drunk.

"None of my teachers were ever that pretty," Jack complained.

"Mine, neither," Brian agreed.

The two men toasted their mutual deprivation.

Kat sighed as she pulled her pen from her hip pocket. "Here's my number," she said, neatly printing the seven digits on the grainy white surface of a napkin. "Call me tomorrow. I want to research the black dye on the Internet. If it's too risky—"

He cut her off. "It's my risk, and I'll sign a paper abslo...absov...absolving—tough word—you of any responsibility."

She was curious about why this was so important to him, but she knew better than to ask in front of another guy. Not if she wanted a truthful answer.

"If you want to buy Brian's so-called black henna, that's up to you. I'll let you know my answer in the morning. But I don't have a cell, so you'll have to call before ten if you want to set something up."

"What happens at ten?"

"I take my son to his summer arts program. I normally get back around eleven, though, so I could probably fit you in then."

"Can you do more than one tattoo?"

"I have a folder full of designs. The price depends on the complexity and how long it takes."

"No problem. Do I come to you?"

She gripped her pen a little tighter. Normally she did her work in a booth surrounded by other vendors. She'd done tats at her house for friends and family members, but she'd never invited a stranger to her home before. Nor had she gone to a man's motel room. The second image felt a bit too sleazy. "I guess that'll work. We can do it on the deck. I'll give you directions when you call."

That seemed to work for him. He carefully folded the napkin and put it in the pocket of his jeans. She turned to leave, but a hand on her wrist stopped her. "I don't know your last name, Kat."

"Petroski."

He repeated it slowly, as if committing it to memory. She happened to look at his lips as he murmured the syllables and a tingle coursed through her body from the top of her scalp to the tips of her toes.

A direct hit of swoo.

"I'm Jack Treadwell," he said, offering his hand.

She swallowed a gulp of courage. *He wants to shake your hand, not kiss you, you idiot.*

She squared her shoulders and held her breath as she gave him her hand. She tried not to notice how smooth and warm his skin felt. Not sweaty as Drew's had been the first time he touched her—pulling her to her feet after accidentally bowling her over on the softball field. Or rough from working on engines the way Pete's were to this day from his hobby of building hot rods. One quick, firm shake, then she yanked back. "Gotta go. If you don't call, I'll assume this yearning to get tattooed was the Jäger talking."

"Oh, I'll be there. One more thing to cross off my list."

She knew all about lists—goals. She was one semester away from realizing a dream she'd set for herself when she was ten. She wanted to be a teacher and change people's lives. The way Mrs. Findham—her fifth-grade teacher—had changed hers. Lois Findham. The first person to see Kat's potential and praise her efforts. To a child caught in an emotionally brutal custody tug-of-war, the positive attention had given Kat a smidgen of hope.

Not that Kat's path had been quick or easy—thanks to the reckless choices she'd made—but she was so close to the end of the tunnel she could almost shout with joy.

And shout she would this coming December after she completed her student teaching. In the meantime, the extra cash this R.U.B. was offering would come in handy. And despite the fact that she felt a dangerous level of swoo emanating from him, she wasn't worried. She'd learned her lesson—twice.

This was a business transaction, not a date. Besides, he really wasn't her type. In fact, she didn't even like motorcycles.

JACK WATCHED Kat for a few moments longer as she made her rounds. A bright spot in an otherwise stereotypical bar decorated in an Old West style that was probably far, far from the real thing. He considered himself fairly well versed in Old West history and legend— enough to know that the facts behind the legend often got blurred in the retelling for the sake of the story. He didn't expect to see much of the *real* Old West here— at least not during this hectic celebration, but he could buy a forest-service map and head into the Hills. Do some exploring. *Wind up lost.*

He wasn't sure whether the voice in his head was his mother's or Jaydene's. Frowning, he took a drink from the glass of water the waitress—Kat—had brought without him asking. It was cold and delicious. He hadn't realized how parched he was. Maybe he was also drunker than he'd thought. Kat had seemed to think so when she'd urged him to get some supper.

"So, how 'bout a fricken…shicken…fried chicken steak?"

Brian chortled. "Okay." He dug in his pocket for what Jack hoped was money, not car keys.

"Lesgo," he said, tossing a ten on the table.

Jack added another twenty just to be safe. He'd lost track of their bill several rounds ago. He looked for Kat to thank her and confirm their meeting the next day, but she was nowhere to be seen.

The disappointment he felt surprised him. She was pretty. And nice. But that didn't mean he'd ever give in to the attraction he felt for her. He'd made it a rule never to date women with children. He didn't like kids. It didn't take a psychiatrist to figure out why. His father's career as a dentist—and his life—had been ruined by a lying, conniving child who had been coached by his greedy, low-life parents to say Jack's father had touched him inappropriately. And since Jack's dad had been performing the dental procedure on a weekend—free of charge—to an underprivileged child, there hadn't been any staff or dental assistant to say otherwise.

Jack had been fifteen. Even in a city the size of Denver, the rumors had gotten around. His once respected, beloved, community-minded father found himself defending his honor, his veracity and his livelihood. The team of lawyers that represented his father's insurance company had pushed for a settlement to avoid the cost of a jury trial. They'd argued that the scandal would blow over faster—and his family would be saved the humiliation of appearing in court and hearing the allegation voiced against him—if he agreed to settle.

Money changed hands. The charges were dropped. His father was never the same. Nobody was.

All because of a lying little brat.

Jack paused in the doorway of the bar for one last glance over his shoulder. With any luck, she wouldn't look as cute and appealing tomorrow when he went to her house to get yet one more thing crossed off his list. Dull and unadventurous Jack was going to get a tattoo. Sort of.

He told himself if he liked the looks of it—and the way it made him feel—he might get the real thing done later on. Changing his image might be the first step in changing his life. Maybe Jack would no longer be a dull boy.

Maybe.

CHAPTER THREE

"HI, MOM."

Kat looked up from the washing machine, where she was fishing for a gray sock plastered like a leach to the enamel basket. The voice wasn't the one she'd been expecting. She'd heard a car pull into her gravel drive and the sound of the neighbor's dogs barking—an early-warning system she didn't have to feed—and had assumed it was Char bringing Jordie home from his first overnight powwow.

Char had already called twice that morning to explain why they were running late and apologize for missing Jordie's art class. Kat had been quick to assure her that the activity was on a drop-in basis, so Char could take her time. "Keep him," she'd teased. "I had the house to myself last night. You wouldn't believe how well I slept."

A lie. She always returned from work keyed up, so she'd spent several hours online researching PPD, contact dermatitis and other side effects of so-called black henna.

"Tag!" she exclaimed now. "What are you doing here? Are you okay? Did something happen?"

Her son heaved his disappointed-old-man sigh—that was what she called it—and dumped his backpack on the peeling vinyl flooring. "Aiden got poison ivy. Him and Dad are meeting Michelle at urgent care. Dad said I could come home, instead of hanging around the waiting room for who knows how long. I'm gonna see if there's anything on TV."

He didn't ask for permission, nor did he offer her a hug. He used to. Until last year. She really hated the distance that came with growing up.

"Not so fast, young man." She ripped a dryer sheet in two and tossed one half into the dryer. "Give your mom a hug or she'll hide the remote."

He rolled his eyes but complied.

He smelled awful—sweat, campfire, musty sleeping bag and fish—and wonderful. She squeezed him tighter than she knew he liked and as expected he protested with a groan. "Mo-om."

"Sorry," she said, plucking a twig from his white-blond hair. He was growing it long—to get his dad's attention, she figured. His father hated long hair, of course.

A horn beeped.

"Dad wants to talk to you."

To apologize for inconveniencing her by bringing Tag home early? *Yeah, right.*

She exited the door Tag had just entered and crossed the five-foot-by-four-foot porch her landlord euphemistically called a patio-slash-deck. It had been tacked to the double-wide modular home before Kat moved in, and in his opinion warranted an extra seventy-five dollars worth of rent. Kat didn't agree, but she paid it, anyway because the location provided easy access to both Sentinel Pass, the town she called home, and the northern Black Hills communities of

Lead, Deadwood and Spearfish where she worked and went to school.

She took a deep breath of fairly cool morning air as she trotted down the slight incline to the driveway. "Hey, what's up?" she asked, rising on her toes to look inside the older Ford Explorer. "Not feeling so hot, Aiden?"

The boy in question, slim and dark-haired, was strapped in a booster chair in the backseat. Although the same age as Jordie, Aiden had his mother's slight build. Michelle was half-Korean, and Aiden had thick black hair and dark brown eyes. Nobody who saw Tag and Aiden together believed they were half brothers.

The child shook his head and squirmed uncomfortably, although Kat couldn't see any visible evidence of red patches on his skinny arms or legs.

"It's around his butt," Pete said, as if reading her thoughts. He looked more irked than sympathetic, but it was hard to tell, thanks to the two-day growth of stubble on his jaw and neck. A neck that had thickened considerably in the years since their divorce.

"He had to take a crap when he and Tag were hiking and he used leaves to wipe."

"Ooh." Kat cringed, remembering when something like that had happened to Tag. His genitals had become so inflamed he'd had to sit in a special soak for several days. "That's too bad, Aiden. But it'll go away with the right medicine."

Twin tears welled up in the boy's eyes and his bottom lip started to quiver. Kat knew her ex-husband well enough to know he wasn't cutting Aiden a lot of slack.

Pete made a face when he looked in the rearview mirror, but he didn't say anything. The scolding would come, Kat knew. Pete was as emotionally distant as Kat's father, which was one reason she'd divorced him.

"I'll be back for Tag in a couple of hours," he said. "I figured he'd be better off here than hanging around a waiting room."

She agreed, but she didn't appreciate Pete's treating her like a drop-in child-care center. "You should have called first, Pete. What if I wasn't here?"

He shrugged. "You know what reception is like around Deerfield Lake. It was faster to swing by. If you weren't here, I'd have just taken him with me."

"I might have had plans."

He put the car in gear and eased back a few inches. "Do you want me to take him or not? I really don't have time for this, Kat."

Well, neither do I, she wanted to shout. But she didn't. Shouting was what her parents had done. Every time one had dropped her off at the other's house there'd been shouting. She'd promised herself she wasn't going to do that to her children—even if it made her look like a doormat.

"He can stay, but keep your cell phone on. If I have to meet Char to pick up Jordie, I'll drop Tag off in town." She didn't mention her potential tattoo client.

"Whatever."

She waved at the sad little tyke in the backseat. Pete was always hardest on those he loved most, but how do you explain that to a six-year-old?

She watched the car drive off, wondering as usual if she could have done things differently where both her ex-husbands were concerned.

"Mom," Tag called from the porch. "Jordie's on the

phone. He wants to stay longer with Char. He said he's learning how to make arrowheads. How come I can't do that? I never get to do anything fun."

Kat had to work to keep a straight face. "You were fishing and camping, remember?" she asked, dashing back to the house. She took the phone from his outstretched hand. "Char took Jordie to the powwow because I worked last night. You know that."

His bottom lip stuck out belligerently, but she sensed that his disappointment stemmed more from not being with his father than from not attending a Lakota festival. He shrugged and walked back into the living room, where he had a video game set up.

Kat hopped up on the washer and put the phone to her ear. "Hello, son. Are you having a good time?"

"Yeah. It's cool. We ate Indian tacos last night."

Jordie loved food. "Mmm. Sounds yummy. What else have you been doing?"

"Swimmin'. And dancin', 'n playin'." He bubbled on about his various activities in a way that made her smile. Her younger son was most like her, and the tenderness she felt toward him had the ability to bring her to tears at the strangest times.

"I'm glad you're having fun, honey. Can you put Char on? I don't see any reason you can't—"

"Okay. I haffa go. We're gonna make arrowheads. Bye, Mommy."

"Bye, honey boy. I love you."

There was a loud clunk followed by a laughing voice. "Wow, Kat, that kid is hell on wheels. How do you keep up with him?"

"I don't. That's why I sent him with you," Kat said,

smiling. She slipped off her perch and tucked the phone under her ear so she could stuff another load into the washer. How two boys who had to be bribed to bathe could go through so much laundry was beyond her. "I fully expected you to be sick of him by now. Are you a glutton for punishment or what?" She and Char were close-enough friends to know when the other was kidding.

"He's having a lot of fun and everything is fine at the shop so I thought we'd stay another day, if you don't care…."

"That's fine, Char. As long as you're not sick of him, I'm fine with you keeping him another night. I'm a little surprised," she said. Major understatement. "But…"

"I know," Char said. "I expected to be exhausted at the very least, but he's a great kid, Kat. Really easy to be around, and the other children have sort of adopted him. Like a junior mascot or something."

Kat could picture it. Jordie was very good at blending in. Something he got from her, she figured.

"Hey," Char said. "I forgot to ask you earlier. How'd you do on tips?"

Thanks to a certain tipsy R.U.B. she'd made double what she usually took home. "Pretty good. Enough to get my radiator flushed."

Char chortled. "Keep talking dirty like that and I'll kick your kid out of my tent in favor of some young stud."

Kat smiled. Big talk from someone who practically qualified as a nun. Their mutual friend Libby theorized that something in Char's past had caused her to protect her heart with a fierceness that scared away most men.

"Jordie loves money. Maybe you could hire him to sell raffle tickets for the chance to woo you."

"Woo. Sounds closely related to your swoo. No thanks. So, what are you going to do with a night off by yourself?"

"That depends on whether or not Pete comes back for Tag."

"Huh? What happened to the fishing trip? I thought that was supposed to last all weekend."

Kat explained about Aiden's medical emergency.

"Oh, man, that sucks. Sounds like a trick a big brother who knows what poison ivy looks like might have pulled on a littler kid he isn't crazy about."

Kat hadn't considered that. "You're right. If I'd been more outdoorsy as a child, one or more of my half siblings probably could have sucked me into falling for that. I'll ask, but I hope for Tag's sake he didn't. Aiden's mother would make his life more miserable than usual if she found out."

Pete's second wife, Michelle, tended to be very protective of her two children, Aiden and baby Cassidy, to the exclusion of her stepson. Kat gave Pete credit for including Tag in family outings as much as he did, because she was sure Michelle didn't make it easy for him. Or Tag.

She and Char talked a few minutes longer. Char had spoken to Libby the night before and had the latest scoop on another mutual friend and book-club member, Jenna Murphy. Jenna and Libby were in California at the moment but were due back soon.

"So it looks like we're still on schedule for our regular meeting," Char said. "You're hosting, right? Tell me the title of the book again. I'll stop by the mall on the way home tomorrow."

"*Water for Elephants*. You'll love it. I promise."

They hung up a few minutes later without Kat disclosing the fact that she'd scheduled a tattoo at her home. Maybe because she didn't do impulsive things that involved strange men she met in a bar and her friend would assume Kat was desperate for money—which she usually was. But she preferred to think she didn't mention the tattoo because more than likely the handsome R.U.B. would be a no-show. He hadn't called, after all.

A good thing, she told herself. She didn't have time for men with potentially lethal swoo. Not when she was so close to finally getting her life on track. And as her mother had proved more than once, nothing could derail a great plan faster than the wrong man.

Kat had just set down the phone when it rang. Her hand shook slightly as she snatched it up before Tag could get the extension. If this was the biker named Jack, she preferred not to have to explain the call to her son.

"Hello?"

"Um…good morning. Is this Kat?"

"Yes."

"I'm Jack. We met at the bar last night. By the way, thanks for trying to keep me from making a complete ass of myself. I'm sorry about that incident with the Three Stooges woman."

She snickered. "Mo. How's your jaw?"

"A little sore, but I think I have you to thank that I'm still talking this morning. Was that guy she was with as big as I remember or is that the booze talking?"

His humility and embarrassment seemed in direct contrast to Pete's attitude. "He was rather large."

"That's what I thought." He paused. "So, um…are we still on for that tattoo?"

She swallowed the lump that suddenly thickened in her throat. *He's a client. Free money. You can do this.* "I printed out the information about the black dye. This is nasty stuff and it can cause some really bad reactions. I'd like to go on record as one hundred percent against the idea of using it, but if you're supplying the ink, I'll give it a try. No promises."

"Great. Brian dropped the stuff at the front desk this morning. Apparently he handles his liquor better than I do, because I could barely open my eyes until about an hour ago."

She liked it that he was honest about his hangover. Most men of her acquaintance would have pretended they could handle anything.

"I'll do it, but I have a small change of plans. My son came home early from his camping trip and his father could show up at any time to pick him up. Since I'd planned on doing it outside...well, if having an audience makes you uncomfortable, we might have to reschedule."

He didn't answer right away. "How old is your son?"

"Eight. He'll be nine in September."

There were a few seconds of dead air, then he said, "You'll be there the whole time, right? I guess it's okay."

She didn't understand what he meant by the comment but assumed he'd asked about Tag's age fearing she might need to juggle a toddler on her hip while applying the tattoo. "Do you have a pen handy? I'll give you directions to my place. Say at two?"

"Perfect."

He listened without interruption until she mentioned the turnoff for Sentinel Pass. "If you see a big white tepee, you've gone too far."

"Sentinel Pass? Is that the town where some film crew is supposed to be making a movie? Brian was talking about it last night."

Rumors had been flying ever since Libby's new husband, Cooper Lindstrom—a popular TV personality—had arrived in the area in response to Lib's online ad. And once Jenna's boyfriend, producer/director Shane Reynard, showed up a few weeks later, the truth had gotten splashed all over the newspapers.

"It's a television show, not a movie," she told him. "A half-hour sitcom. And the actual onsite filming isn't starting for another week or two. My friend's fiancé is the director."

"Cool. Never watched a TV show being made, but I'll be back in Denver by then."

A good thing to remember, Kat told herself. In case his swoo started to get to her. A very good thing.

JACK WONDERED why nobody warned him that the roar of a motorcycle engine magnified the pain of a hangover. The noise and vibration traveled up his spine making his brain feel as if it might explode inside his helmet. He'd meant to take another handful of painkillers before he left his hotel room, but a call from his mother had thrown him offtrack. Now he had to hurry or he'd be late for his appointment.

"Stop acting like a petulant little boy," his mother had scolded. "Jaydene will come around eventually."

Come around. The irony of her word choice would have amused him if he hadn't been slightly nauseous from the greasy meal he'd consumed the night before.

"Mother, as I told you before I left Denver, Jaydene

and I are history. She wants a different kind of life than I do." One that involved multiple sex partners.

"Oh, for heaven's sake. She's a senior loan analyst on the fast track for my old job. You're an orthodontist with a flourishing practice. I introduced you to Jaydene for a reason."

Until that moment Jack had forgotten that his mother had set him up with Jaydene. He'd arrived for dinner one night at his family home and had found a stranger at the door. A striking, thin brunette in very high heels.

In his gut, Jack had known for some time that something wasn't quite right between him and Jaydene. For one thing, he didn't share her fascination with provocative, sexually themed paintings and sculpture. For another, she talked constantly—especially when they were making love. Giving directions or being verbal about one's pleasure was one thing. Carrying on a thrust-for-thrust play-by-play got old, in his opinion.

But his mother had claimed the two were perfect for each other, and Jack tended to humor his mother. Partly out of habit and partly because his father had demanded it. "Your mother's word is law around here, son. She's smarter than both of us put together. What Rosaline says goes."

Well, Jack was sick to death of bossy, manipulative women. He was on a motorcycle in the middle of nowhere to prove to himself that he could make decisions without benefit of a committee. This meant taking risks his mother would abhor and his ex would admire.

If he survived the bike ride to Kat Petroski's house.

When he'd finally opened his eyes that morning, he'd told himself he was going to call her to cancel. Only a total schmuck would consider getting a fake tattoo. But the thought of numerous needles pricking his skin made him queasy. He hated needles so much he wouldn't undergo even the most benign dental procedure without complete sedation.

Was there some kind of subconscious link between his fear and his feelings for his dentist father? His sister seemed to think so, but Jack didn't like to dwell on the past. His father was dead, so any anger or disappointment he harbored toward the man was a waste of energy.

Still, one thing Jack had learned from hanging out in the bar so long last night was that no amount of alcohol could numb his anxiety enough to make him get a real tattoo.

A fake one was going to have to do.

And if he were being honest, he wanted to see Kat again. If for no other reason than to assuage his curiosity. She'd appeared in his dream early that morning. A winsome spirit with a lute that she claimed she couldn't play. "I'm looking for a man who can make my lute sing," she'd said.

"Is that a clever way of asking for sex? Did my ex-fiancée send you? What is it with you women? Is sex all you ever think about?" he'd railed at her from the fence he'd been sitting on.

She'd cocked her pretty head and grinned. "I bought this lute for my son and I need to find a teacher. If I wanted to have sex with you, I'd say so." Then she'd licked her bottom lip and given him a suggestive look that made him wake up with a woody.

Juvenile. Silly. He attributed his distressed libido to the fact he hadn't had sex in four months. At least he hoped that's all it was. She really wasn't his type. And he planned to remember that even if her kids weren't around when he got there.

He passed one garishly colored billboard hawking some kind of tourist trap called the Mystery Spot, then half a mile later he saw the sign Kat had mentioned. It featured a giant white tepee set against a bright blue sky. Native arts and crafts for sale. Four miles ahead at the Sentinel Pass turnoff.

He eased off the gas and looked around. He didn't want to have to backtrack.

Nice area, he thought, starting to take stock of the scenery. The highway wound through the middle of a wide valley bracketed by pine-covered hills to the right and a red-capped bluff of some sort to the left. The homes spread out along the road seemed hedged in by the escarpment.

Jack didn't think he'd enjoy living someplace that could be mowed down by an avalanche come winter.

"You worry about the most improbable things, Jackson," Jaydene once told him. She'd always used his given name, instead of his nickname. She claimed it was more dignified.

As soon as he spotted a split-rail fence leading to a steep driveway, he put on his blinker and checked over his shoulder to make sure it was safe to turn. He was still getting used to the feel of his bike, which was both fast and vulnerable.

A cacophony of barking dogs greeted him as he veered to the right toward a small, but neatly maintained manufactured home. No animals came out to nip at his tires, but the noise didn't let up until he turned off the engine. He put down the kickstand and got off. His butt felt tingly and a little sweaty. Something else they didn't tell you when you were bike shopping.

The sound of a door slamming made him turn toward the house. A young boy flew down the steps and raced to where Jack was parked.

"Sweet ride, man," the kid said. "Are you lost?"

"I'm looking for K—"

"He's in the right place, Tag," a woman's voice said from the porch. "But he's half an hour early."

Jack looked toward the house. Kat. Barmaid. Woman of his dreams.

"This guy's here to see you, Mom? Why?"

"He's a customer from the bar last night. I'm giving him a tattoo. Like I do at the street fair," she added, obviously trying to make his presence no big deal. "I just talked to your dad, Tag. He's on his way here."

"With Aiden, too?"

Kat shook her head. "No. His mom's keeping him home. You're sure you didn't have anything to do with what happened?"

"Mom!" the boy exploded. "I told you. Aiden went into the bushes to take a dump. He didn't ask me for help."

She stared a moment, lips pursed. "I believe you. I just hope he doesn't decide he needs someone to blame."

Jack watched the exchange with interest. If he'd ever raised his voice to his mother like that, she'd have had a bar of soap in his mouth so fast he wouldn't have had time to blink. She also wouldn't have trusted him so easily.

"Children lie," she'd told him years later when his father's accuser recanted his testimony. Too late to help his father regain even a small bit of what he'd lost.

"Your father learned that the hard way, son. I hope you're not as gullible."

Being accused of molesting young boys was bad enough, but being known as the son of a pedophile who beat the rap had its own sort of horror. And add to that the fact Jack's wisdom teeth came in early, making his canine teeth shift forward.

Kids lied. They could also be very, very cruel.

"Hey, Fang Boy, how do you suck cock with vampire teeth?"

"If your daddy did it, you must diddle little boys, too, right?"

Jack had grown up fast. The first thing he did when he went to college was get braces, using the money his late grandmother had left him. He was so happy with the end result and how it made him feel about himself, he opted to specialize in adult orthodontics, instead of family dentistry.

"Fixing a patient's bite is one thing," his father had argued. "Messing with what God and genetics saw fit to produce is not our place."

Jack knew his father secretly had hoped Jack would revive the Treadwell family practice after he graduated, but Jack had other plans. He didn't like kids, and he would never willingly put himself in the position of being alone with one.

"Don't touch the bike," he told the boy, who was squatting a foot or so away, studying the bike's engine.

"I ain't gonna hurt it."

"I know. Because you're not going to touch it, right?"

The kid—Tag, his mother had called him—looked ready to make a smart-ass comeback, but he didn't get a chance because his mother shouted from the porch, "Taggart John Linden, get up here this second. You are *not* going anywhere until you clean up this mess."

The boy's upper lip curled back and he muttered something Jack couldn't hear, but he sprang to his feet and dashed away like a young gazelle.

Jack was tempted to get back on his bike and leave, but as he reached for the key in his pocket, he heard Kat say, "I'm ready for you."

Her sweet tone was so far from provocative only an absolute, hard-up idiot would be turned on by it, but suddenly he didn't want to be anywhere else.

CHAPTER FOUR

IT TOOK KAT a few minutes to get things set up to her liking. She needed space to move around and visualize her canvas. Not that she considered herself an artist. But she had great respect for the history of henna art and she always tried to do her best for the customer.

"This is the first time I've had a client come to my house," she said, studying the placement of the straight-back kitchen chair she'd brought outside.

"Really? Does that mean you're a virgin, too?"

His voice was kind of scratchy—the ways hers was in the morning after she worked at the bar. But she had no trouble discerning the humor he'd intended.

"Yep, That's me," she teased back. "Both boys were the product of immaculate conception. Or so their fathers would like to believe," she added softly.

"Divorce is never easy. My sister went through a tough one last year. No kids, fortunately."

She pointed to the chair for him to sit down. "Yeah. Emotionally you already feel like a failure, but with kids in the picture you have to deal with their fear and guilt and hurt. It's tough."

He started to say something else, but she unfurled the drop cloth she would use to protect the deck with a crisp crack. Divorce wasn't the best topic to discuss before starting a tattoo. Just thinking about her failures made her tense and unhappy.

"So, you're from Denver. Nice city."

He gazed at her a moment before shrugging his surprisingly broad shoulders. Had they gotten wider and more masculine overnight?

"It's home."

"You have family there?" Not too obvious, right? She assumed he was single, but assumptions had gotten her in trouble in the past.

"My mother lives about a mile from me in one direction and my sister's half a mile or so in the opposite direction. No wife or kids. I was engaged until a couple of months ago."

Aha. "You traded your fiancée for a Hog."

His smile looked pained at first, then it brightened. "And I got the better end of the deal, too."

She chuckled softly as she opened her kit—a modified, plastic fishing-tackle box. "No bitterness, I see."

"The breakup was a good thing." His slight hesitation made her think this might be the first time he realized that. She could still recall the exact moment when the truth about her choice to divorce her exes hit home.

"Well, good," she said. "You have a fresh start, a road trip and, soon, a temporary tattoo to take home with you."

She stepped back and looked around, satisfied that everything was the way she wanted it, then handed him a plastic binder filled with laminated sheets of designs. Some pages included photos of the work she'd done on other clients. "Pick out which designs you'd like me to do and I'll quote you a price. Take your time. I'm going to check on my son."

Kat hurried inside, not liking the lack of noise she heard coming from Tag's direction. Her son wasn't above pouting until the last minute, then racing through whatever chores needed to be done—especially if he knew she was in a hurry. "Tag?"

He wasn't in the living room, but she was relieved to see that the video game was off and the snack plate he'd used earlier was no longer on the floor. She hurried down the narrow corridor to his bedroom. "Tag? Are you ready? Your dad should be here any minute."

She knocked once, then opened the door. The image of Tag standing at the window watching for his father was so sad and familiar she had to clap her hand over her mouth to keep from crying out. She couldn't count the number of times she'd stood just like that. Waiting and wondering. *Will Mom remember? Or will she be so busy with the other kids she forgets about me?*

Kat was the only child her mother shared with Kat's father. Kat's half siblings included two older children from her mother's first marriage and two younger kids from the guy she married after she divorced Kat's dad. And the web of extended family—some blood relations, some not—on her dad's side was just as complicated.

There had been times in her life when Kat felt like a jackalope—the mythical animal that was half jackrabbit, half antelope. She not only looked different from all of her half siblings, she always felt strange and unwelcome.

"Something wrong, kiddo?"

"I don't like him."

"Your dad?"

"That guy. The one on the motorcycle. He's a fake, Mom."

She vacillated between wanting to praise his insight—Jack wasn't an authentic biker—and feeling compelled to correct his manners. "He's a client, Tag. A stranger. And we have no right to judge him."

Tag turned to face her. "Dad won't like him, either. He might make us stay here until you're done giving him the tattoo."

"Your father doesn't have any say in what I do, Tag, and I'm not a fool when it comes to taking risks. This guy isn't dangerous."

After hearing the story of Jenna's rape in college, Kat wasn't about to take chances. Plus, she'd worked in bars long enough to sense the dark side of people. Jack Treadwell might be a little down on women at the moment, given his recent breakup, but he didn't seem the type to turn violent.

"Maybe not, but Dad isn't going to like him."

Kat didn't really care what her ex-husband thought, but she didn't want Tag to stay awake all night worrying. She picked up his bag and motioned him to follow. "Come on. You can wait on the porch with us until your dad gets here. Maybe if you talk to Jack, you'll like him better."

"He's a—"

"Don't say it. Whatever *it* is. You know the rule."

Tag rolled his eyes and muttered under his breath, "If you can't say something nice, don't say nothin' at all."

"Anything," she corrected. "Come on."

He followed behind her with enough distance to make it appear he was leaving the house on his own, not because his mother made him. She dropped his bag on the top step, then picked up her duplicate order form and pen and turned to face her client. "So, what's it going be?"

Jack looked up, apparently so engrossed in his choices he hadn't heard her return. His eyes were an unusual shade of gray, which made her want to study them. He glanced down and pointed to a design on the page. "You've done some really nice stuff here, Kat. What a pity they wear off eventually. Have you ever considered doing the real thing?"

She kept one ear on her son's faltering footsteps. "Not really. This is a hobby. To do it professionally I'd have to get more training, and I already have a career in mind."

"Teaching?"

She blinked in surprise until she remembered Brian mentioning her major the night before. "That's right."

"Body art might pay more," he said, his tone wry.

"That could be true in a state like South Dakota. Next door in Wyoming, starting salary for a teacher is almost 10K more."

"So you're planning on moving after you graduate?"

The screen door opened.

"No. I'll be happy just to have summers off to be with my boys. I'm not going anywhere. Tag and Jordie love it here." She motioned Tag to come closer. "I don't think you two were formally introduced. Jack, this is my son, Taggart. Tag for short. His brother is at a powwow with friends."

Jack leaned forward to shake Tag's hand. "Good to meet you. Your mom said you're going camping. Cool. Not something my father ever did with me."

Tag's hand looked small and grubby next to Jack's. And something about the image made Kat's eyes well up. She tried to hide her embarrassment by hurrying Tag off. "Wait on the step, honey. That way your dad won't have to honk and get the neighbor dogs all riled up." *Or get out to give me grief about my client.*

To her surprise, Tag didn't argue.

Once he was seated, she looked at Jack and said, "So, which did you choose? I think you said you wanted a couple, right?"

"This strand of barbed wire around my upper arm, for sure," he said, flipping back a couple of pages in the binder. "And what about this one for my neck?"

She'd had an idea which she thought would look best and was pleased when his choice matched hers. "Good," she said.

She was close enough to see his cheeks color a bit at her praise. She found his blush terribly sweet. And took a step back.

Sweet and swoo were a dangerous mix. "Anything else?" She tried to keep her tone stiff and professional.

He gave her an odd look but quickly skimmed ahead to one of the upper-torso shots. "This one caught my eye right off the bat."

She felt her eyebrows shoot upward. "Really?"

"What's wrong with it?"

"Nothing. It's one of my favorites, but I don't do it a lot because it costs quite a bit. And takes me nearly an hour."

"Is time an issue?"

She glanced at her wrist. No watch. She'd forgotten to put it on. "Um…I guess not. Henna takes longer to dry, so that adds to the overall time, but if you're sure about using the black…"

"Yep. Positive." He reached down and picked up a brown paper sack. "I read the printout you clipped to the binder, but nothing in the report has changed my mind."

Again, she wanted to ask why, but didn't feel comfortable probing into personal matters in front of Tag. "I'll give the ink a try, but no promises. We'll start with your arm. If it comes out okay, then I'll try another."

"Excellent," he said with a smile. "If it works out, I'd like this one right here." He poked a spot to the right of his heart.

She stepped closer and leaned over to see which image he was pointing at. A rose with a thorny stem and tears dropping from the points. The image cried, "Back off and leave my broken heart alone." At least that was what she'd been thinking when she'd drawn it.

Bloody thorns. A surefire swoo stopper.

"You got it," she said, suddenly feeling much better about her decision to do this at home.

A second later, the neighbor dogs started barking.

"Dad's here," Tag called.

"Uncharacteristically good timing," she murmured before dashing to the steps to give her son one last hug. He indulged her—probably to make up for earlier— then he hurried away, clomping down the steps in a noisy descent.

She stood for a moment, then waved when she saw father and son look her way. She didn't hang around to see if Pete wanted to talk to her. Instead, she walked straight to her supply box and picked up her bottle of mehlabiya oil. She'd already decided to follow her usual procedures even if she agreed to try a different dye.

"I need you to take off your shirt, then scoot the chair

closer to the railing. You'll lean forward and rest your right arm like so," she said, demonstrating.

"No problem." His words were muffled and when she looked at him, she saw that he was in the process of yanking off his T-shirt. Arms lifted, he struggled a moment, his bare chest and torso displayed with heart-stopping clarity.

He was a perfect blend of Pete's leanness and Drew's roundness. And most women would have killed for that skin tone. No visible tan lines. "Do you go to a tanning salon?" she asked, without meaning to say the words aloud.

Once his head was free, he looked at her. "Pardon? Tanning? God, no. Too busy. But I swim laps. Heated pool, so I can do it year-round."

A swimmer's shoulders. Of course. She should have known. Pete had been on the water-polo team in high school when they first started dating.

She cleared her throat. "Can I get you a glass of water or a pop before we start?"

"Water would be good. My body is definitely dehydrated after all that booze last night. I hope I didn't make too big a fool of myself."

She shook her head. "I was afraid I might have to tattoo over bruises today, but luckily Mo and Curly left pretty quickly."

His chuckle was low and intimate. Kat was sure he hadn't intended it as sexy, but her body reacted as if it was. Damn. He wasn't making this easy. But she was determined to stay detached and professional. Even if she had to hang out in the kitchen a few minutes and practice yoga breathing.

"Get settled. I'll be right back."

Jack watched Kat walk away. Well, walk wasn't the right word. She seemed to bound with natural grace. She was a petite ball of energy, and he liked her. Her kid he could live without. Sullen. Even with his back to the adults, Jack had sensed the boy's animosity.

My fault, he thought. *I could have handled things better where the bike was concerned.*

But what he didn't know about kids could fill more pages than Kat's tattoo portfolio. And he was okay with that. There were plenty of women around who didn't have children. Maybe not quite as many who didn't *want* children, but if he kept looking he'd find one.

Someday.

In the meantime, he could appreciate Kat as a woman and an artist. He didn't know why she didn't regard herself as an artist, but the sketch he'd picked for his back was gorgeous. A Celtic cross with ivy and some kind of lily entwined around it. He'd been drawn to it immediately, and expected to pay dearly, although she hadn't named her price yet.

"Hey, Kat, you were going to tell me how much. I want to be sure I have enough cash. I'm assuming you don't take credit cards."

She returned a moment later with two large acrylic tumblers filled with ice and water. The one she handed him had a straw. "This way you can drink without moving your neck," she told him. "When I start on your back."

After she sat her glass on her worktable, she passed him an invoice with his total bill circled at the bottom. "How's that look?"

Cheap. He'd add a healthy tip to bring it up to what

it should be. "No complaints." He handed it back. "I have the cash in my pocket. Do you want it up front?"

She shook her head. "Let's make sure they turn out the way you hoped. Now, for the last time, are you sure I can't talk you into real henna? It's a centuries-old tradition and the color is really beautiful as it fades." She frowned. "Technically, the dye is permanent. The reason it disappears is your body grows new epidermis and sloughs the dyed cells off."

He shook his head. "If the chlorine in the racket club's pool doesn't affect me, nothing will. I swear on my life I won't sue you if Brian's stuff leaves a scar. Do you want me to sign some kind of consent form?"

"I would if I had one," she said, releasing a deep breath. Her sigh had the unintentional result of reminding him of his dream. He took a drink through the straw to ease the lump in his throat. He needed to keep his focus on something other than her charming little body, her smell, her touch. It wasn't going to be easy, but small talk might help.

"So, tell me more about this Hollywood thing. Are they hiring locals to be extras?"

She put her hands on the outside of his shoulders to get him squared up the way she wanted. He felt tilted slightly to one side, but his view of the hillside was less provocative than watching her move. The reddish dirt reminded him of home. He'd done his share of hiking around Red Rocks.

She used a piece of fabric to wipe the area where the tattoo would go. Her touch was firm and practiced.

"Extras?" he prompted.

"Oh, yes. Sorry. I was visualizing this design and got

distracted. The TV show. Right. They are hiring people. My friend Libby put my name at the top of the list."

"I've never been around a movie or television set. They're not doing this for a couple of weeks, you said?"

"Uh-huh. I don't know the exact date."

"But you signed up?"

"Well…um…sure. I can always use the money. As long as the filming doesn't fall during the Sturgis Bike Rally."

The guy he'd bought his bike from had urged Jack to attend the event. "Motorcyles like you have never seen in your life, man," the guy had raved. "And the partying. Totally crazy."

Jack had purposely planned this trip to avoid the mayhem. A fact that would have made Jaydene laugh since his attitude seemed to support her contention that he was antisocial and unadventurous.

"You attend the bike rally?"

"Have for years. I can do a couple of grand's worth of tattoos when the bikers are in town. A lot of their lady friends want the look, but not the permanence. I do body piercing, too."

He tried to look over his shoulder to where she was squatting. "Really? Maybe I—"

She used the heel of her hand to push his head back down. "Piercing involves needles. No way around it. Now, sit still. I'm sketching in the gap from my stencil. Your biceps are pretty well developed for a dentist."

For a dentist. A general assumption he'd come to expect. His wasn't the most glamorous of occupations, but as a little boy he could still recall how proud he'd been when his father came to the school to inspect his classmates' teeth. Free. "Just doing my civic duty," his dad would say humbly.

Years later—after the accusation and brouhaha—people had speculated about his father's motive for volunteering to do the school exams.

Jack closed his eyes and concentrated on the strange feeling of a pen lightly dancing across his skin. The heat from her hand was there, too. The sensation was utterly sensuous and hypnotizing.

He wasn't sure how or when, but the next thing he knew Kat was shaking his opposite shoulder. "The first one is done, but I think we're going to have to move inside before I do the one on your back and your chest. The wind's come up. Feels like rain."

Rain? Not a good thing for a biker.

He blinked and sat upright, a little groggy from his nap. "I fell asleep."

"I know. Happens all the time. The applicator works like a micro massage or something."

His embarrassment eased. He picked up his shirt, but she grabbed it from him. "This ink is drying fast, but not that fast. Why don't you go inside and check out the design in the mirror? See if the black ink is living up to your expectations."

He stood, covering his yawn with his left hand. She held the door open for him. "The bathroom is straight ahead, first door on the left."

The vanity was spotless, but also jam-packed with juvenile toiletries—boy kind. A comic-book hero toothbrush. Some other action-figure soap dispenser. Two hairbrushes. Two tubes of toothpaste. Neither was the kind his father would have approved of.

He turned sideways. The image on his bicep was larger, and much darker, than it had looked in the picture. The black seemed to shine like newly spilled tar. He assumed the brilliance would fade pretty quickly. What surprised him was how vibrant and dynamic the design looked when he flexed.

"What do you think?" she asked from the doorway.

"I'm beginning to understand why people get tattoos. This is great. I love it."

"Phew," she said, wiping an imaginary bead of sweat from her smooth brow. "I'm glad. The gothic barbed wire has a lot of detail."

He looked at her in the mirror, standing close enough for him to see but not close enough to actually make contact with him. He found it funny that she remained so aloof after she'd just spent twenty minutes touching him. He wondered if her edginess was because of the small space he'd inadvertently invaded.

When her gaze met his, he saw for the first time just how blue her eyes really were. Like a Rocky Mountain lake reflecting the sky on a sunny day. Gorgeous.

She quickly retreated and motioned for him to proceed ahead of her. "We should probably get to the others right away. I want the ink to have time to dry before you take off. It could be a problem if you got caught in a storm."

He looked around as he returned to the kitchen. The living room was small—about the size of his office waiting room—but every bit as neat as the other parts of the house he'd seen. Probably a tough accomplishment with two young children. He could see stacks of board games under the coffee table and what looked like an Xbox or some video-game apparatus. Although his office manager stocked several of the latest games for their younger clients, Jack had never owned one. His father hadn't approved. He thought video games created fat, lazy kids.

Kat's son wasn't fat. Jack couldn't speak to the kid's ambition.

"How do you feel?"

"Fine. Although I'm a little embarrassed. I can't tell you the last time I took a nap."

"It was after eleven when you left the bar."

"And then I stuffed myself with chicken-fried steak. It was delicious, by the way." He even took a photo of the monster-size plate covered in white gravy. Rib-sticking, a heart attack on a plate, as he'd heard people say.

He lowered himself onto the straight-back chair that Kat had carried inside. "Let me put this pillow on the table. Rest your forehead on it and put your hands in your lap. Do you think you can hold this position for half an hour?"

"I'll try."

She cocked her head as if surprised by his answer. His sister often accused him of being too honest. "Girls like a little mystery, Jackson. You don't always have to spell everything out in black and white."

Maybe, but hyperbole wasn't his style. Which was why he felt compelled to set the record straight where Kat Petroski was concerned. "You know I'm not an experienced biker, right?"

She looked up from the binder she'd brought into the kitchen and set on the counter beside the sink. "Pardon? Oh, right. I already guessed that."

"Because the bike looks new?"

She danced a fingertip across the fabric of his jeans. "Your leathers aren't broken in. But, hey, you have to start somewhere. It's not a comment on your ability to handle the bike or anything."

She picked up her stencil and leaned forward. The smell of ink and something delicious, like oatmeal cookies, filled his nostrils.

Damn. Between her touch and her scent he was going to be lucky if he managed to keep from making a fool of himself. He turned his chin so he could see the door of the refrigerator. A small collection of school photos were grouped in one corner, with the rest of the space devoted to art projects and papers. A spelling test with a big red A-plus on it. A kid's pencil sketch of trees and a very large bird, probably an eagle.

He couldn't remember his mother ever hanging a single thing he or his sister produced anywhere in the house. She wasn't the sentimental type, his father once told him. "Mom lives in the moment. It's a good place to be."

But at the moment, soft hands were touching his back and a faint breath tinged with wintergreen drifted across the hair on the nape of his neck. Gooseflesh formed across his arms.

"Are you chilled? I can close the window. Probably should, anyway. Sometimes the rain doesn't give you any warning."

"I'm fine. Maybe you should skip the one on my chest. Would you believe I left my rain gear in my hotel room? Talk about unprepared."

She shrugged. "Worst case, you can put your bike in

my shed and I'll give you a ride to Deadwood. I need to pick up my check from the bar."

"You're not on duty tonight?"

She leaned down to his level and shook her head. The saucy curls bounced. Up close he could tell the sun-streaked colors varied from very light cream to burnt gold. He'd never been drawn to blondes, but that bias didn't seem to apply to her.

"I was filling in for a friend last night. I'd work there more often—the money's good—but finding a sitter is always a challenge."

"What about your sons' father?"

"Fathers. Plural. Two boys. Two ex-husbands. And as much as I'd like to say Pete and Drew are totally committed to making sure their sons' mother gets an occasional break, I'd be lying."

He couldn't help but smile. She didn't sound as if she expected things to be any other way. He wondered why.

"Can't you write that kind of arrangement into your custody papers?"

"Oh, that's how things started out, but life intrudes. Younger siblings develop rashes. Stepmoms have second and third babies. Schedules change, and since I remember what it's like when divorced parents bicker, I try to keep things on an even keel for my boys. Even if it inconveniences me."

He found that commendable. Heroic, even.

He'd been thinking a lot about what constituted a hero. Even before he knew for sure he was coming to the Black Hills, he'd read about some of the local characters, like Wild Bill Hickok. Was his enduring fame due to the circumstances surrounding his untimely death? Or did his legacy stem from a code of honor he'd held to dearly until that fateful night in the Number Ten saloon?

Jack wasn't sure, but the idea of exploring off the beaten path came back to him. "How long have you lived in the Black Hills?"

"All my life. I was born in Spearfish, but between my parents' divorce and my own marriages, I've lived all around. Custer. Sturgis. Belle Fourche. Rapid. You name it, I probably lived there."

"So, if I wanted a tour guide who could show me the *real* Black Hills, you'd be the one to hire, right?"

She bent down to his level again. "I've never done that before."

"Would you be interested?"

"Do you mean I'd drive you around in my car?"

He shook his head. "On my bike. It came with an extra helmet. You could give me a running history of the area and tell me where to go."

She frowned slightly as if thinking over the proposition. "When?"

"Tomorrow? If it doesn't rain."

"Well…Jordie is supposed to go to his dad's tomorrow for a week, and Tag has another two days of camping scheduled, so I suppose I could. But I couldn't do it for free."

"Of course not." He did some quick math. Eight hours. Forty dollars an hour seemed fair. He quoted her the price.

"Seriously? Deal."

She flashed a bright smile, then quickly ducked her head and went back to work. "No more talking. You're making my ink dry too fast."

He was careful not to chuckle. Didn't want to move and ruin her artistry.

He wasn't an impulsive kind of guy, but in two days he'd made two big, impulsive gestures. So far, he was very satisfied with the first. He only hoped the second would prove equally smart.

After all, there had to be worse things than riding around the mountains with a beautiful blonde on the back of his bike.

CHAPTER FIVE

"READY?"

Jack couldn't hear her voice over the roar of his engine, but he read the word on her lips. Her pretty pinkish coral lips that glistened in the morning sunshine. The storm had blown itself out during the night and the day looked very promising, Jack thought, turning off the deafening rumble of his engine.

He removed his helmet and got off the bike. In the background, her neighbor's dogs barked with a furor that surely would have meant dismemberment if they were loose.

"Enough," Kat shouted in the dogs' general direction. The barking stopped.

"Nicely done," Jack said. "You're going to make a great teacher."

She seemed pleased by his remark, but she didn't acknowledge it. Instead, she repeated, "Are you ready for this?" She patted her purse, which had enough straps to qualify as a backpack, too. "I picked up a bunch of promotional fliers in case you change your mind about doing the tourist thing. And I have a really detailed forest-service map, too."

Something he'd been thinking about buying. Jack

liked that she seemed to be taking her role as his guide seriously. That made the arrangement seem less like a date. Which it definitely wasn't. He couldn't afford to date her, not after last night's dream. Another sizzler.

He bent to retrieve the spare helmet he carried. "Sure am. Everything square with your sons?"

She nodded but didn't elaborate. Maybe she sensed that he wasn't really into kids.

"I listened to the weather report and it looks like you caught a break. Hot and sunny all day."

The storm he'd ridden home in the day before had produced a mere sputter of precipitation, but the strong headwind had left him chilled to the bone, despite his leather jacket.

He'd spent the rest of the evening under the covers, his nose in a book he'd picked up at the convenience store. The more he read about Seth Bullock, local lawman-turned-entrepreneur, the more intrigued he became about the man behind the myth. According to the book, he'd founded a town in 1890. Maybe they'd have time to visit Belle Fourche, too.

"I'm ready for a little heat so I can show off my cool tattoos," he said, running a finger along the neckline of his T-shirt. He was careful not to touch the actual tattoo, even though he felt the urge to scratch it. Kat had been adamant about keeping his hands off it. "Shower with warm water, no soap. And pat dry," she'd said.

"I thought you might be thinking that, so I brought along some sunscreen," she said, holding up her bag.

He opened one of the side compartments. "Great. Drop it in. I'll put some on later. I've been cooped up indoors way too long and need a little color."

She hesitated—the mother in her probably wanted to slather him down, anyway—but after a moment tucked her bag into the space. She shook her head lightly before donning the helmet. The sun made her hair sparkle with white-gold highlights he had a feeling were completely natural.

As she tightened the chin strap, he studied her. For a small woman, she was nicely proportioned with a little extra padding where it counted. Her bright yellow tank top appeared to have a built-in bra because he couldn't see another set of straps. Her faded denim jeans fit her like a second skin. On her feet were well-worn hiking boots, and tied around her waist was a long-sleeved white shirt.

A man's shirt, he could see by the label when she turned to walk to the bike. Probably belonged to one of her husbands, he thought, frowning at the unsettling sensation in his belly. Why should he care if she still wore a former husband's shirt?

"So where are we going first?" he asked, throwing his right leg over the seat and scooting forward to give her room to get settled.

"You have two choices—north or south. I suggest south. Sylvan Lake. The Needles Highway. Harney Peak. If you're up for a hike, you'll get a fabulous view of the entire Hills."

"How long does it take to get to the top?"

Even though she wasn't snuggled against his back, he felt her shrug. The sensation made him all too aware of her. This could be a long day, he thought.

"I can't remember. I haven't done it in a while," she said.

Me, neither.

As if realizing her comment could be misconstrued, she added too quickly, "Four hours, I think. Up and back. Depending on how fast you are. I mean, how fast you walk." Her groan made him smile. "Can we go now?"

"Good idea. I think I'd rather ride than walk, but I'll let you know when we get there, okay?"

She nodded so vigorously their helmets clicked.

He looked down to make sure her feet were on the pegs, then he started the bike. When her hands settled lightly on his waist, he felt their warmth permeate his whole body the same way her touch had yesterday. It was a reward in and of itself. He didn't understand it and told himself any woman's touch would do the same thing to a guy who hadn't had sex in months. But a part of him knew that wasn't true.

Shifting sideways enough to make eye contact, he asked, "Can you hear me?" He tapped the side of his helmet near his ear.

Her smile showed pure delight. "Wow. That's perfect. I was expecting some crackling walkie-talkie thing. And I can hear music in the background. Daughtry. One of my favorites. How'd you know?"

He didn't want to admit that he'd seen the name on a list on her table yesterday. He'd downloaded it to his MP3 player last night. Probably a dumb gesture, given he'd never see this woman again after today, but he'd done it, anyway.

"Are you an *American Idol* fan? It's one of the few shows the boys and I agree on. Although that's not something they'd tell their fathers."

Jack didn't ask why. He knew why. There'd been hundreds of things he didn't tell his dad. And vice versa. Especially the big stuff.

"Turn left when you leave my driveway," she said, leaning into him, even though she didn't need to in order to be heard. "I hate crossing traffic, but it's fairly light this time of day."

"For the height of summer, I've found the traffic pretty tolerable. Especially compared to Rocky Mountain National Park."

"You won't say that when we reach Hill City," she said with a low chuckle that wormed its way into his very core. "And there's always a crowd around Mount Rushmore."

He checked both ways, then gunned it. The bike shot across the road smoothly. Kat resumed talking once they were up to speed.

"If we're not hiking Harney Peak, we can afford to take our time. I can show you some of the back roads, since you said you were interested in history. If this were a four-wheeler, there are all kinds of places I could take you."

He didn't doubt that for a minute. He could think of a few that weren't on the map. But the thought disappeared when the semi they were passing suddenly pulled out to pass the car ahead of it.

Jack swerved to the shoulder and cranked on the gas. The bike shot ahead and easily cleared both vehicles, but the sensation of flying, along with a rush of adrenaline, made his entire body tingle. "Holy crap," he muttered. "That semi driver must not have seen me. I flashed him, too."

Kat's heart felt squeezed to the size of a peanut and

she could barely find the breath to say, "Thank God you have sharp reflexes. That could have been ugly."

"I agree. But you helped by leaning the right way with me. You've done this before, I think."

"My first husband had a bike in high school. He sold it after Tag was born. Broke his heart, he claimed, but I notice he hasn't bought one to replace it."

She sat back and relaxed her death grip around his waist. "For being new to riding, you did that well."

His chuckle was low and masculine. "Thanks. It comes from driving with an inherently high adrenaline level."

Again, he downplayed her praise. His modesty was refreshing, but sometimes it rang false. She was about to test her theory when she reminded herself that she was a paid employee, not a prospective girlfriend. This wasn't a date.

She cleared her throat and looked around, wondering what to point out. A familiar sign made her cry, "Oh!"

She lifted her arm and pointed. "There's the turnoff to Sentinel Pass. We can start your tour there. Hang a right at the big white tepee."

Once they were off the main highway, she inched back. "You better slow down. The potholes are bad enough in a car. On a bike, they'll probably loosen old fillings. Everybody is hoping the new money coming to town will encourage the county to fix the road."

He didn't say anything, but the bike bobbed and weaved until they reached the outskirts of town. Since there was no traffic behind them, he pulled to the shoulder and stopped to look around.

Pointing toward the large purple-and-yellow billboard a few feet away, he asked, "What's the Mystery Spot?"

"Sentinel Pass's one and only tourist trap. My friend Jenna owns it with her mother. Her father was the mastermind behind it. He was also a scientist who taught at the School of Mines during the school year. He died a few years ago. The Spot is sort of hokey, but in a good-spirited way. My sons love it. In fact, Tag—the one you met—was going to work for Jenna this summer, but it didn't work out."

"How come?"

"Too much driving on my part." And considering the price of gas… "He's still mad at me."

"My mother wouldn't let me work when I was a kid, either. Because of my asthma. I don't remember how old I was, but it seemed like everybody I knew had a summer job—even the girls. I felt left out."

That had been one of Tag's arguments, too. "When he has a car of his own, he can work wherever he wants."

"But he won't have as many choices and he won't have had this experience to put on a résumé."

She sat back with a snort. "Why do people who don't have kids always have the strongest opinions about how to raise them?" she asked. "He won't be nine for another couple of months. This so-called job was really my friend's attempt to help me out with child care this summer while giving Tag a chance to earn a little spending money."

"Oh. I see." His chuckle sounded conciliatory. "Sorry. You're right. Not my business. But I do remember giving my mother a hard time for depriving me." He said the word mockingly. "Fortunately, I discovered swimming that summer and my asthma got better. Plus, I was living in a city where I had access to public transportation. So, I'll keep my mouth shut from now on, okay?"

She nodded, embarrassed by her outburst. She wasn't usually so quick to take offense. Ever the peacemaker, her mother used to say.

"Let's cruise through town," she suggested. "I'll point out all the historic spots. Like Seymour, our dinosaur. And the post office where Libby worked as postmaster."

"She's married to what's-his-name…the talent-show guy?"

"Cooper Lindstrom. He and Lib are so much in love it almost hurts to see them."

He put the bike in gear and slowly made the turn. Kat sat up a little straighter, hoping to see someone she knew. How often did a mother of two get to ride behind a handsome guy on an awesome new Harley?

"Why?"

"Why what?"

"Why does it hurt to see them together?"

She hated the way he not only listened, but actually heard what she said. She wasn't used to that. "Um…well—" how honest did she want to be? "—because seeing Libby and Cooper together makes you wonder if that all-encompassing, only-in-romance-novels kind of love is ever going to come your way or if you're going to be a freakish statistic that throws off the bell curve your whole life."

He didn't say anything for a moment, but stopped the bike in the visitors' parking just the other side of the fire station. He turned off the engine and removed his helmet. Kat did, too, even though her cheeks were on fire.

"I want to meet these people," he told her when they were both standing.

"Are you making fun of me?"

He shook his head, but he was smiling, so she wasn't certain he meant it. "I've never seen that kind of love and I want to."

She was still trying to make up her mind whether or not he was kidding when a voice called, "Kat? What are you doing here?"

Kat spun around so fast she almost dropped her helmet. "Char. Why aren't you at the tepee?" They hadn't talked since Char brought a happy, exhausted Jordie home the day before.

"I had to mail a bunch of stuff. Thank God for Internet sales, that's all I can say." She looked from the bike to Kat to Jack and back to Kat. "I told you I've forgiven eBay for screwing up Libby's original ad, right? I mean, why not? It all worked out. And it was partly Lib's fault for thinking she could post an ad without naming an exact dollar figure."

Kat hadn't really paid much attention to Libby's original ad, which had been responsible for bringing her plight to Cooper's attention, but she did know that Char listed a great many items on the online auction site. "I guess… Um, Char, this is Jack…" Her mind went blank.

"Treadwell," Jack supplied. "Nice to meet you."

They shook hands. "He's from Denver. I'm showing him around the Hills."

One of Char's dramatically arched eyebrows lifted. "Starting in Sentinel Pass?"

"Yeah," Kat said, standing her ground. "That's the point, isn't it? All the hype about the TV show is supposed to bring tourists in. Jack's a tourist. He wanted to see the place. Right?"

Jack's enigmatic gray eyes were glinting with humor, but he nodded gamely. "I especially want to see the famous lovers."

Char's explosion of laughter nearly made her drop her fistful of mail. "Which pair? We've got two, you know. This love thing seems to be catching. Might be something in the water. Which is why I drink wine."

Kat rolled her eyes. They'd had this discussion before. Char had made it clear she didn't believe in love, despite her addiction to romance novels. "Libby and Jenna aren't back yet, are they?"

Char shook her head. "I'm picking Jenna up at the airport on Sunday. She said she tried to call you last night and didn't get an answer. Libby and Coop are flying home later. He didn't want her traveling without him. I don't know why. She's pregnant, not an invalid."

Kat knew why. Neither of her exes—or anyone else in her family—had ever worried about her like that, but then, nobody had ever loved her the way Cooper loved Libby. Which probably wasn't surprising. To be loved, first you had to be seen for who you really were.

"Kat?"

Kat blinked, glancing from Jack to Char. "Huh? Sorry. Zoned out for a minute. I was…um…trying to map out our next stop." *Liar.*

"I told Jack if he's still here on the tenth, Cooper is throwing a big party for the town. Everyone is invited."

Libby had mentioned something about a whole-town celebration since their wedding had been so small and rushed to dodge media intrusion. "I didn't know they set a date. Lib said they wanted to coordinate it around the Sentinel Pass filming."

Char shrugged as if that part of the deal didn't interest her in the least. "How's Jordie?"

"Good. I think he's in love with you."

Char kicked her beautifully beaded moccasin against the base of Seymour's pedestal. "He's the sweetest kid I've ever known. If I had a kid, I'd want him to be just like Jordan."

Kat heard a funny catch in her friend's voice, but before she could give it more thought, a horn honked behind them. Char pivoted like a dancer and gracefully loped to the large, dusty four-wheel-drive truck that sat double-parked on Main Street.

"Don't you people work for a living?" the driver hollered good-naturedly through the open passenger window.

Char hopped up on the running board. Kat couldn't make out their conversation, so she turned to Jack. "That's Mac. Libby's brother. He and Lib own the Little Poke gold mine, which is going to be one of the spots the film crew plans to use locally."

Jack looked puzzled. "That truck looks like it's on its last leg. I thought gold was worth a lot of money right now."

"I think you're right, but it also costs a fortune to get it out of the ground. Are you interested in mines? I could ask Mac to give you a tour."

He shook his head. "Naw. That's okay. Dark tunnels don't really appeal to me."

Her, neither. But she couldn't help thinking that his list of phobias was growing. Kids. Needles. Tight spaces. But he knew how to drive a bike. That had to count for something.

Not that she had a mental scorecard going or anything. Nope. She wasn't going to rejoin the dating game till her boys were in high school. Maybe college.

Jack studied Mac's truck a moment, then scanned the street. His expression said he didn't see what the whole fuss was about, but that was probably to be expected since he didn't know Libby and Cooper.

He nodded toward the bike. "We should probably be going, huh?"

"Right." She waved to her friends. "See you later, Mac. Say hi to Megan for me. I'll call you tonight, Char."

"Bye. Nice meeting you, Jack. Hope to see you around."

She felt funny hopping behind Jack with her friends watching, but once she'd made it clear that her interest in the man was purely mercenary, she was sure they wouldn't try to play matchmaker.

Powerful swoo not withstanding, the guy wasn't her type. Even if she was in the market. Which she wasn't.

CHAPTER SIX

ACCORDING TO HIS ODOMETER, they'd traveled just under a hundred miles when the first sense that something wasn't right sank into his consciousness. They'd twined along the Needles Highway—a most impressive and at times confounding landscape. He'd been tempted to change his mind about walking to the top of Harney Peak when they stopped at Sylvan Lake, but by then the morning was almost gone, so he'd chosen to head to Custer State Park, instead.

And he was glad he had. The views were amazing, the road just challenging enough to be able to drive and talk. And the conversation had been heady. Kat was not only sweet and accommodating, she was smart. And she knew her Black Hills lore. He liked it that she didn't buy history's attempt to whitewash reputations.

"Seth Bullock is a perfect example," she was saying, leaning closer as she had every time she had a point to make. Normally, he'd have enjoyed the contact, but at the moment, his skin was tingling—in a not-so-pleasant way—around the areas where she'd put his tattoos. "He was strong enough to hold on to what he grabbed in Deadwood and smart enough to make friends with powerful people, like Teddy Roosevelt. Did that make him a good man? The people who lived in the little town near present-day Belle Fourche—I can't remember the name at the moment—might not have liked him much when he made a deal with the railroad that changed the line from their town to a spot through his land. Sure, he offered citizens of the town free lots if they wanted to move, but what about the ones who'd invested their life savings on a dream that he crushed?"

"I guess the HBO show got canceled before that happened," Jack said, trying to keep from wiggling.

She sighed and leaned into him a bit more. "Yes, well, just because a person is portrayed one way on television doesn't make it the truth. I mean, the actor who played Seth Bullock was excellent. Great eyes. Did you know that one of Seth Bullock's grandsons said his granddad never needed a gun because he had a stare that could stop a bull elephant?"

Jack didn't know that. Nor did he care, particularly. Something was wrong, but he didn't know what to do about it. He'd have to tell her soon if it didn't get better. Luckily, she hadn't seemed to notice anything was amiss.

"And one thing I've learned from Libby's experience is that TV and reality are quite often very far apart. If something isn't entertaining, it isn't relevan—" She paused. "Is something wrong? You seem really tense."

He swallowed. "I think I may need some of the sunscreen you brought. My neck feels a little hot." At least, he hoped it was the sun and not something else making his skin burn.

She pulled back and a second later he felt her fingertip prod his shoulder. Then the nape of his neck where the tattoo started.

He heard her swallow. "I can't see the color exactly because of my sunglasses, but the skin looks a little puffy. Let's stop somewhere for a cold drink and I'll check it out."

A nice ice bath—or jumping into one of the lakes they'd passed—sounded better, but he followed Kat's directions into the town of Custer. A few minutes later, they were seated across from each other at a pizza joint.

"Char claims this is the best pizza in the Hills," she said after taking a long drink from the glass of water the waitress had left with the menus. "How does your back feel?"

He stuck his fingers in his glass and fished out a couple cubes of ice. "It's starting to sting a little. Is that normal?"

He ran the instant relief around the back of his neck, locating the source of the anguish. The tattoo.

He looked at Kat, who was frowning. "If you're having an allergic reaction to the dye, it sure came on fast. From what I read, most reactions happen ten to fourteen days after application. Maybe we should find a clinic to check it out."

He made a scoffing sound. "I told you, I'm not allergic. But even if I were, I don't need a doctor."

She shook her head. "Men. That's exactly the reaction I'd expect from both of my exes. What is it with your gender? Haven't you heard of anaphylactic shock? This could be serious."

"The tattoo itches a little. Maybe that's the way the ink dries. No big deal. Can we order? I like pepperoni-and-mushroom."

"Me, too." Her smile looked conciliatory. "Actually," she admitted shyly, "I like pepperoni and anything."

She pulled out her forest-service map and showed him where they'd been and the road she planned to take back home. He pretended to pay attention, but the truth was growing more apparent by the minute that she was right and he was wrong. Very wrong. The fire was spreading from the tattoo on his back to the others. He wrapped both hands around the tall, red-plastic water glass to keep from scratching the spots that now felt as though an army of ants was setting up camp under his skin.

He shifted his shoulders without meaning to.

Kat's eyes narrowed. "It's getting worse, isn't it."

He slumped back in the booth, sighing as the air-conditioning-chilled vinyl made contact with the burning cross on his back. "My arms and chest are starting to tingle, too."

He waited for an "I told you so," but instead, she got up and walked away. Jack watched her cross the room to the pay phone hanging on the wall. She thumbed through the phone book suspended on a chain beside the phone. Her back was to him when she tucked the receiver under one ear.

She returned to the table at the same time as the pizza arrived. Jack's appetite had waned. Nerves, he figured. He hated doctors almost as much as he hated needles. "Thank you," he and Kat both said when the waitress slid the steaming hot pie in front of them.

"There's an urgent-care facility a few blocks away. We can walk there, if you want. The receptionist said it was quiet at the moment and they could see you right away."

He could tell she was serious about having him looked at—probably to protect her own interests, since her tattoo had created the problem. "Nobody ever died of itching."

"One of my half-brother's uncles died of an allergic reaction to shellfish. He didn't even know he had a sensitivity until it was too late."

Jack scowled. "I'm not going to die in the next ten minutes. Can we eat first?"

She didn't say anything. Maybe she was used to men acting like stubborn fools. She sat and slid a piece of pizza onto her paper plate. After a brief pause—to pray or see if he'd changed his mind, Jack wasn't sure which—she started eating.

She ate with gusto. Jack would have, too, if he could have kept his mind on chewing. He tried, but it was no use. The problem was a problem.

When the waitress returned to check on them, Jack had no choice but to ask for their bill and a take-out box. Kat pulled some extra napkins from the dispenser and offered to leave the tip.

He had to give her credit. He didn't know a single person who wouldn't have said, "I told you so."

Forty minutes later, a young doctor with an English accent gave Jack the news. "Beautiful work. Too bad you're allergic."

"How is that possible? I've never had a reaction to anything."

"You've probably always been allergic to whatever was in that ink. You just never got exposed to it before now. I can give you a shot to keep your symptoms from getting worse, and I'll prescribe a cream to help with the itching."

"Am I safe to drive my motorcycle back to Deadwood?"

The man's face scrunched up. He consulted his watch,

then sighed. "Generally it's best not to drive or operate heavy machinery after taking this shot. You will probably feel drowsy within the next half hour or so. Your wife is in the waiting room, correct? Can she drive?"

Jack didn't want to explain who Kat was, so he merely shook his head and said, "We're both on the bike. She doesn't have a motorcycle license."

"Well, then, I suggest you get a motel room in Custer, have your wife fill the prescription I'm going to give you and tuck in for the night."

Jack swallowed and let out a sigh of frustration. The cost of guide services was definitely going up.

"I'M AN ADULT, Char. The man is sick. The drugs knocked him flat. He's not a threat and there are two separate beds in the room. I'm perfectly safe."

Kat had called her friend after a great deal of soul-searching. She'd weighed her other options—catching a bus, calling one of her half siblings for a ride or hitting the street to find another room—this motel had only the one left when they'd registered. In the end she'd decided to take the path of least resistance. She'd sleep in the spare bed in Jack's room and beat him into submission if he tried anything fresh. Not that he could. He was out cold from the shot he'd been given.

"I only have one thing to say to you, Kat," her friend replied. "What would Libby do?"

Kat smiled for the first time in hours. She felt miserable. Responsible. And pissed off. She should have listened to her intuition and refused to use that crummy old ink. She planned to throw it in the toxic chemical recycling as soon as she got home.

"Well, Libby got knocked up by a man she barely knew. Are you sure we want to go there?"

Char's laugh eased a bit more of Kat's tension. "Good point. Hey, you're a responsible adult and the guy's swoo is completely nonfunctioning, right? Along with certain important body parts, I gather. So why exactly did you call me? Permission? Or confession?"

"Neither, you goose. I wanted to let someone know where I was in case Jack wakes up in the middle of the night and murders me."

"Hmm…maybe I should come after you. Custer's not that far away. I could be there in an hour after I close up."

Kat sighed into the small phone. Jack had insisted she use his cell to make her arrangements. "If you can find someone to pick you up, I'll pay for their gas," he'd said. "This is completely my fault and I feel like a total schmuck." Not something either Pete or Drew would have admitted.

"No," Kat said to Char. "Don't change your plans. He's already sound asleep. I bought a book in a gift shop down the street. I'll read until I can't keep my eyes open, then sleep in the chair."

"I thought you said there were two beds."

"There are, but it just struck me that I barely know the guy, Char. I'm not that comfortable around him."

"You looked pretty comfy behind him on that bike."

Kat wandered to the railing and looked at the motorcycle parked below the second-floor room. She had felt at ease with Jack until he started to show signs of an allergic reaction. She blamed herself, even though she'd tried her best to talk him into using henna.

"He's a nice guy. Smart. Funny. But still a guy. When I tried to talk him out of using that damn black ink, would he listen? Heck, no. He's as bullheaded and single-minded as either of my exes." She let out a sigh. "I'm starting a new chapter in my life, Char. One that doesn't depend on a man to make me happy, fulfilled or even to pay the bills."

"I know, Kat. And I'm pulling for you, but the guy is pretty cute. So unless you tattooed his pecker, he might be able to get it up. If you're there, anyway, what would a little safe sex hurt?"

Kat's bark of laughter made two strangers strolling along the sidewalk look her way. She ducked her head, blushing. "You're almost as bad as Jenna. She says the most outrageous things."

"And look how things worked out for her. She wound up with a great guy *and* a dog. I'm just saying, think about it and keep your options open. A lot of places have complimentary condoms at the front desk. You could ask. In case he makes a sudden, perky improvement."

Kat rolled her eyes. She was a mother. She hadn't had sex in…well, a very long time. She might consider some friendly, noncommittal sex once she completed her degree and had a job. Movies and sex every other Saturday night with a single coworker or something. But she sure as heck wasn't going to jump the bones of a perfect stranger who was nearly comatose from an allergic reaction she'd caused.

Shaking her head, she said good-night and tucked the phone in her pocket. She'd left the door slightly ajar so she could quietly slip inside.

"Is your friend coming? Did you tell her I'd buy the gas?"

Kat licked her lips and walked to the bed closest to the bathroom. Jack was stretched out like a man staked to die in the sun. Before going outside, she'd applied the thick white cream to his tattoos, which now resembled shiny black etchings outlined by a raised foundation of brilliant-red flesh. He'd stripped down to his navy blue shorts but had modestly pulled the top sheet up to the middle of his chest.

"She can't come. I told her not to break her plans because you weren't in any shape to attack me if I stayed here."

He opened his eyes and turned his head slightly. "My mother likes to believe she raised a gentleman. Her number's on my phone under 'Mom' if you need reassuring."

That made Kat smile. He really was a nice guy. Normal. Decent. She'd be fine. "How do you feel?"

"The itching is better, but my brain feels groggy. Definitely a good thing we're not on the bike. But I feel bad about screwing up your night. You didn't have a date, did you?"

Her hackles went up. That was the kind of question Pete would have asked. Before she could set him straight, he added, "I mean, as a single mom, if you have a night off without kids, you have every right to do something fun. And watching a dumb-ass guy who didn't listen to your very sound advice squirm in itchy agony probably doesn't qualify."

Her temper disappeared. "Oh, don't be so sure. I don't get the chance to gloat all that often."

His snicker sounded sleepy and she expected him to start snoring, but instead, he mumbled softly, "Beautiful, smart *and* a sense of humor. Perfect combination."

He thinks I'm smart?

She shook off the small shiver of pleasure his words gave her. "I bought a book to read. The light won't bother you, will it?"

She waited for an answer, but the only sound that came from his perfectly shaped, utterly masculine lips was a light snore.

Smiling, she unlaced her boots, kicked them off and tucked her stocking feet under her as she settled into the surprisingly comfortable wing chair. With a nice fat pillow from the bed under her arm, she got comfortable and prepared to read about the early pioneers' attempts to bring social structure to the raw, turbulent towns of the pre-annexed Black Hills.

She loved the subject matter, and the author's writing was intriguing, if not gifted.

But the sun and wind and fretting over Jack's condition quickly caught up with her. Her eyelids fluttered closed and her breathing evened out. Just a quick nap, then she'd watch *Letterman,* she told herself.

CHAPTER SEVEN

THE PEN FELT heavy and awkward in her hand. She couldn't explain why. As a teacher, she'd done her sums in ink ever since leaving school. Miss Marshall, her teacher, had proclaimed Katherine the smartest student and had awarded her a good-conduct ribbon, as well as a brand-new pen-and-ink set she'd gotten from back East.

The pen remained one of Katherine's most prized possessions. Perhaps because, from that point on, she'd felt as if her life had controlled her and not the other way around. Her parents had convinced her to move with them to the frontier where teachers were in short supply.

But so were doctors. And when the influenza came, it took them both. And her younger siblings.

Thank the good Lord above that she had a job, or else her life could have been much, much worse. She'd managed to save enough money from the tiny stipends she earned to keep the land her father had claimed—until the railroad came.

Of course, they'd paid her pennies on the dollar for the claim her father had given his life to procure. And her strident voice—a lone, strident voice, it seemed— against the bullying tactics of the railroad had cost her her teaching position. The board of citizens voted to find someone less confrontational. But they gave her a good recommendation to assuage their lily-livered consciences.

And so she'd answered an advertisement for a teacher in the Dakota Territory town of Deadwood. Room and board provided.

"And did it ever once occur to me to ask if the room included walls that kept out the snow in the winter and grasshoppers in the summer?" she murmured under her breath.

She'd sat down beside the small hearth of her dilapidated home to compose a list of complaints. Money abounded in this mud hole they called a town. She'd seen the gold for herself, spilling from a cloth bag gripped in the stiff fingers of a corpse that very morning. The man's body hadn't been discovered by the vermin some called men, or he surely would have been naked, as well.

She'd done her civic and humane duty and gone to the sheriff—a brooding hulk of a man who terrified her just a hair less than his gun-toting friend. The man they called Mad Jack. Not to be confused with Jack McCall, the infamous idiot who killed the town's most talked-about resident, Wild Bill Hickok.

Sheriff Seth Bullock and Mad Jack—she had no idea if the man had a surname or not—disposed of the body, but not before sharing a smoke and nudging it with the toes of their filthy boots. She'd gone home in disgust, planning to begin the search for a new position in another town. Even Kansas City would be better than here. Possibly Denver.

She had nothing holding her here—even though she'd grown to care for her students. But how could she possibly expect to make a difference in a place where life was so cheap and decency so far from anyone's mind?

She began to write. As was often the case when she was composing, she became so absorbed in the process that she lost her connection with the world around her. She didn't realize the door behind her had come open until she felt a cold shiver trace down her back. She twirled and saw him standing in her doorway.

Her heart climbed into her throat, making speech impossible. She gripped the pen as if to use it as a weapon. A study in futility. The man was known to have survived numerous gunshots and knifings. Death by pen? The thought made a nervous giggle bubble up and slip past her lips.

He cocked his head slightly in a way that most women probably would have found attractive. In fact, Katherine did find him attractive. In a self-destructive way that she was too smart to let sway her.

"I knocked," he said, his deep, smoke-roughened voice filling the tiny space.

"I didn't answer, but still you entered."

"I told Seth I'd check on you."

"Does that make you a dutiful friend or a curious interloper?"

"I lope pretty well. Or rather my horse does." He closed the door and took a step closer.

Close enough for her to see the hint of humor in his eyes, which she noticed were the color of smoke. What an odd thing to notice when she was about to be violated.

At least she assumed her time had come. Men who dealt with death so cavalierly surely would have no qualms about committing rape.

But his attempt at humor confused her.

"What is it you want, Mr....?"

"Jack will do." He looked around. "Small place. Cold, too. You should have better. Maybe if you had a husband. A family."

"I had a family. They died. If I had a husband, he'd have probably caught gold fever by now and be up some gulch with a pan and a rocker."

His gaze returned to her and he studied her as intently as he had her accommodations. She employed all her resources to keep from squirming like a bug being tormented by a bully. No, she thought, that was the wrong analogy. His gaze wasn't harsh or dissecting. It took her apart but not cruelly.

"Rocks—even the kind with gold in them—aren't something that holds my attention. Learned that a long time ago. If I'm gonna gamble my time away, I prefer to do it with cards. The odds seem a little more even."

"Why?"

"There are a lot more rocks than there are cards in a deck."

She couldn't help but smile. But she wished she hadn't when he seemed to take her expression as an invitation to move closer. He was only a step away from where she was sitting. The room, which served as bath and kitchen, as well as sleeping area, was totally inappropriate for entertaining. Especially for a single woman and a man who was not a family member.

"You shouldn't be here," she said as teacherly as possible.

"I know. But I find I'm powerless to make myself leave. Until today I hadn't realized how beautiful you are. And strong-minded. You didn't approve of how Seth and I handled the situation with that body, did you?"

"I did not. You treated the deceased with less respect than most people would have given a dead dog. Your attitude has made me reconsider my place here. If the town's elected officials—"

"Nobody elected me to nothin'," he said, his voice rising. "We saw to the body as best we could. Did we wring our hands and mutter a prayer for his soul? No. Because, frankly, that body is the fifteenth I've helped Seth deal with since I got here. Old. Young. Sick. Gunshot. Murdered. Hung. Run down by a wagon. Every death—friend or stranger—adds another layer between you and fear. It's the only way to keep the blackness at bay."

Strangely, she understood. She'd cried when her mother passed. After giving birth five times, Mama's body had been the most worn down and susceptible to the fever. But as the others succumbed, Katherine had slipped a sort of fine kid glove over her heart. Layer by layer until she didn't feel any pain. Or anything at all.

She couldn't say how it happened, but wordlessly, she rose and went into his arms. Strong, sinewy arms barely cloaked by the coarse material of his coat. He smelled of snow and smoke. He smelled like a man. It had been so long since she'd inhaled those scents up close. They carried with them powerful memories. Her father washing up after a day of working the earth. Her brother sneaking in after courting his beloved Isabeth. Her mother handing her the baby to dry off after he tumbled in the creek behind their home.

She'd missed the touch of these strange male creatures. Her father's hand of support on her shoulder. Her brothers' hugs. Men had courted her, at times. She'd held hands with one or two and danced her share of reels. She'd even kissed Jeremiah Conroy before he headed west to seek his fortune. But she'd never felt drawn like this—a horse to the proverbial water. And she knew, deep down, that she would drink as much as she could take in.

"You are soft in all the right places," Mad Jack told her, his hands taking liberties no man had taken before.

"And you are not. But I sense a softness in your heart that I expect very few people see."

His low chuckle made a shiver course through her body, opening wells of feeling she'd never known existed. Her mind, thankfully, had stopped thinking about all the bad things that could—and probably would—come of this encounter. Propriety and honor were words that lived outside this moment, outside this room.

What mattered now was the roughness of his beard against her palms as she framed his face with her hands. He'd shaved that morning. She could tell. But the outline of stubble told her he was the kind of man who could grow a beard in a week, if he were so inclined.

"How is it that you don't favor a beard in winter?" she asked, bringing her cheek to his. She rubbed back and forth, enjoying the sharp but soft bristles.

"I do when I'm away from camp, but barberin' seems right when you're seeking the company of a lady." He reached behind her, his fingers skimming lightly over the pins that held her tightly twisted bun. "May I?"

She nodded. The only answer possible and one that seemed silly, given how many rules she'd already broken. But the moment his fingers scraped upward, loosening the heavy mane from its braid, her fate was sealed. The pleasure was instant and overwhelming. She put her lips to his. Primly. Puckered. The way she'd learned that one other time.

His answering touch was so different, so powerful and invasive, her heart stopped as his tongue parted her lips and entered her mouth. Was this normal? But the question barely had time to cross her mind before she answered back, her tongue seeking, tasting, exploring.

She was so preoccupied with the sensations she was experiencing in this new and strange arena, she didn't notice at first that he'd managed to remove her outer jacket and was working on undoing the buttons of her shirtwaist. "Oh," she said with a small gasp. "Of course."

He looked at her with a dangerously handsome slant to his mouth. Did he expect her to push him away? That would be the smart choice, but it was not her intention.

"My mother explained that when a man and woman have physical relations, men often prefer the woman to disrobe."

He threw back his head and let out a roar of laughter that both pleased and mortified her. She felt the heat that had been in other places flood her cheeks. She turned away, but he caught her shoulders and made her face him. "You are the most honest, forthright woman I have ever met, Miss Katherine. You don't belong with a man like me, and I've spent every day since you arrived in this godforsaken place trying to stay away from you. But we're here now, and I want you to know that you can trust me.

"I might not have much in the way of land or goods,

but I have my honor. My reputation. I don't cheat at cards. I don't shoot men in the back. And I don't lie to women."

"You didn't laugh because I'm naive and unworldly?"

"No, ma'am. I laughed because you are real and good—two things I never expected to *find* in this godless land, much less touch."

She finished unbuttoning her shirtwaist and went on to remove her skirt and the extra layers of petticoat she'd added for warmth. Her small stove was almost out of coal, but the instant his hands touched her, the heat within her body more than made up for the room's chilly temperature.

He shed his clothes just as fast and pulled back the quilts on her bed. The mattress was lumpy but the sheets fresh from her Sunday washing. He climbed in first and pulled her down so her body was stretched out atop him. She felt exposed and awkward. Her buttocks bare for the world to see—if the world had been looking. But then his large, rough hands covered her nakedness, squeezing her flesh in a way that sent liquid desire to a very specific crux between her legs. She wriggled in response.

"Not too much movement too fast, my pretty kitten. I haven't been with a woman in a long time. We don't want this to be over before we start."

"I don't know what to expect exactly or what's expected from me," she admitted, sharing a confession she'd never said aloud before, even though there had been so many times she'd doubted her abilities, her intelligence, her right to call herself a teacher.

"That's how we learn, my dear, and I would be honored to be your teacher."

So, she became the student. He slowly explored her

body and taught her to trace the same map across the hollows and valleys, plains and hills of muscle and bone of his. He touched her in the most intimate way possible and showed her how to experience pleasure she'd never expected.

"Oh!" she cried when he touched the pulsing, engorged spot in the mound of her feminine seat. That was what Mother had called it, but Mother hadn't said anything about the intoxicating—almost painful—release that came from a steady manipulation of the tiny button. "No more. I don't think I can stand to go there again. Beautiful though it was."

He smiled and gave her a look that nearly stopped her heart. "Honey Kat, that was the outer door. Beyond lies another world you'll want to visit time and again."

She didn't believe him. If that were true, her female friends would have talked about it. Her mother would have said something. Unless she'd never visited such a place. Maybe you only reached that world with someone like Mad Jack. A rogue. A scalawag. A—

Whatever other name she'd been about to call him was lost the moment he flipped her on her back and pressed himself against her. His male part was touching her female part at almost the exact placement of her lovely little button. She tested the fit by wiggling her hips.

The corners of Jack's mouth curled upward. "Now you can wiggle all you want, love."

"Except you're heavy."

He raised up slightly, but that lessened the pressure on her new favorite place. She reached behind him and put her hands on his buttocks. The muscular mass flexed

and he shifted forward slightly. "Good," she said, closing her eyes.

She focused on the feelings, not the mechanics, and
the voice in her mind that seemed to know what came next
told her to open her legs. She did, even though that meant
Jack's manhood fell between them. But opening wider
solved the problem. He pumped his thighs slightly and
the obstacle in question found an opening made for it.

"This might hurt for a minute."

He sounded so apologetic she started to say, "It's
okay." But before the words could form on her lips, he
gave a quick, solid push and was inside her. There might
have been pain, but she was too startled to think about
it. The sensation of a foreign body sharing space with
hers was too unnatural, too frightening.

"Easy, there, love. It's okay. Trust me. Everything
starts to get better now. Rock against me. Move a little
and you'll feel it."

She did trust him. Enough to shift her hips.

"Uh. Oh. Yes."

He nodded in agreement but his eyes were closed and
he appeared to be concentrating very hard. So she closed
her eyes, too, and focused on what she was feeling.
Color. Heat. Need.

The latter urged her on, searching for something she
couldn't name. She moved with an urgency that didn't
seem natural until suddenly it was as natural as breathing. And her breath was gone. Lost in an explosion of
sensation that left her panting.

He'd told the truth. A door had opened to a new
world of wonder and hope. The kind of place you prayed
you'd go to when you died.

Maybe that was why he'd been so cavalier earlier about the dead man. Because Mad Jack knew there were alternatives to living. Some were just more permanent than others.

CHAPTER EIGHT

JACK AWOKE incrementally, and not without some regret. Damn, he'd had a great dream. He couldn't remember all of it, but certain images were crystal clear. The sex. He couldn't name another time he'd come that hard. And the woman in his arms had enjoyed it, too. No faking of that orgasm, he thought with a satisfied sigh.

"Umm-um…"

He opened his eyes at the unexpected sound, which hadn't come from his lips. His heart rate sped up as he looked around, trying not to make any movement.

Strange ceiling. Room-darkening curtains that cried cheap motel room. Extra-firm mattress that didn't feel familiar. And a warm, naked body curled up beside him.

He turned his chin to the left, halfway expecting to see long blond curls. But no. The head resting on his outstretched arm belonged to a real woman. Not the schoolmarm in his dream. This bed-head coif stuck up in every direction. She looked so adorable he couldn't help but smile.

Kat.

Even though he wasn't sure how she'd gotten from the other bed to his. Or wait. Had he been the one to switch?

He looked to his right. "Oh, crap," he muttered softly.

A second messy bed—the one he'd started the night in—was just beyond his fingertips. A cold shiver passed through his body. There was going to be hell to pay any minute.

As if picking up his disquiet, his bedmate stretched and wriggled in a way that made him horny as hell. For half a second. Then, she opened her eyes and blinked.

He felt the instant she realized where she was and that another person was right beside her.

"Oh, my God!" she exclaimed, scrambling sideways, dragging the covers with her.

Her look of abject horror was so obvious Jack felt naked and exposed as the sheets slipped off his body. Rather than fight her for control of the covers, he vaulted into the second bed and yanked the comforter to his waist.

His reaction pissed him off. That was exactly what Jack Treadwell would do. Mad Jack, the person he'd been in his dream, probably would have stood up and proudly walked to Kat's side to calm her down and maybe make love to her again.

He looked across the distance between them to where she sat, pulled into a tight ball of knees and eyes that had the proverbial deer-in-headlights look—right after making contact with a bumper. Too wide and not quite believing what happened really happened.

"Kat, I'm sorry." He wasn't. Not really. But it seemed like the right thing to say. "I don't know what happened. Or how. Exactly. I mean…I don't remember crawling into your bed. Maybe the meds…"

"I… We… Oh, shit. We did more than sleep together, didn't we?"

He nodded, praying the sense of jubilation he still felt

didn't show on his face. "Yeah, we did. Although…" He shut his mouth. Telling her that he'd actually made love to another woman in his dream probably wasn't a good idea. "I… Um… We… I'm sorry?"

She didn't appear to be listening to his pathetic apology. She pulled the sheets away from her chest and looked down, as if checking to see that her body was in one piece.

Jack couldn't help feeling a little offended. "It was straight sex. Nothing kinky. Just ask my ex. I'm as white-bread boring as it comes. No pun intended. I didn't hurt you. Did I?"

She looked at him, her face screwed up in either pain or horror. He wasn't sure which. "I can't believe I did this."

"We," he corrected. "We did this. There were two of us—at the very least," he added under his breath.

Her eyes narrowed. "Oh, that is so typical. Sex is just sex to guys, but I am not in the habit of jumping into bed with strange men. Or—" she whipped her index finger back and forth between his bed and hers "—letting strange men climb into bed with me. How did this happen?"

He could mention his dream, but he didn't think she'd buy his excuse that he wasn't himself. That he'd become an Old West gunslinger named Mad Jack. "Like I said. Maybe the drugs. I could have been sleepwalking." *With a six-gun on my hip.*

A laugh percolated upward, but he tried to cover it with a cough.

"Do you think this is funny?"

"Um…no? No. I don't."

She put her head in her hands and groaned. "Oh, God, not again. Please. Not this time. Not this man. No, no, no. It can't be."

"Hey, Katherine, I mean, Kat. Is your real name...? Never mind. Um, look, I know you're upset, but would you please not act like there's a dead body on the floor?"

She looked up sharply, her hands falling to her lap. The sheet dipped slightly, making it hard for him to remember what he was supposed to be saying.

He cleared his throat and made himself look into her eyes. Her clear, blue, gorgeous eyes that were swimming with tears. He wished he could hold her and comfort her, but he knew she didn't want that. "Kat, what happened was a mistake. Unplanned. Unpremeditated, I promise. But it's not a huge deal, right? I mean, we're both single, and I can fax you my clean health record when I get home. I had a full workup a couple of months ago and haven't been with anyone since. Until last night."

She used the corner of the sheet to wipe her eyes. "Why?"

"Why what?"

"Why did you get a full checkup?"

"I wasn't sure I could trust my ex-fiancée."

"Because you thought she might sleep with a stranger? Like I just did?" Her voice cracked, and he acted on his impulse to comfort her. Mad Jack would have.

Leaning between the beds, he spotted his navy blue shorts and quickly pulled them on. Advancing one knee at a time, he approached her. "Kat," he said softly, lightly touching her arm. "I don't remember exactly what happened. How we got together. How I came to be in your bed. In fact, the last thing I remember clearly is watching you read. Your lips make this kind of fishy look. It's cute." He tried to demonstrate.

Her upper lip quivered in a near snarl and he stopped.

"But the parts I do remember are really good. Hot and passionate. Like an X-rated movie, only with a plot."

She pushed his hand away. "In your dreams maybe."

Maybe. Had he imagined everything? "We didn't have sex?"

She shook her head. "Of course, we had sex. That part was real. I meant your X-rated movie scenario. I don't do X-rated. Ask either of my ex-husbands. I'm too uptight."

"Like a proverbial schoolmarm?"

She let out a little cry. "You're making me crazy. I don't know what happened or why, but it shouldn't have and I know there's going to be hell to pay for it."

He sat back on his haunches. "Why?"

"Because that's the way things happen in my life. Do you want to know my track record? O-for-two. Men were put on the planet to disappoint me. And vice versa, if you ask them. The swoo giveth and it taketh away."

He blinked. "You lost me."

"Better now than later," she said cryptically. Pulling in a deep breath, she gathered her sheet and blanket like a regal cape and scooted off the bed, showing obvious care not to touch him. She paused to pick up her clothes, then hurried to the bathroom. Once inside, she tossed the blankets to the floor and closed the door.

He heard the lock click emphatically.

He blew out a sigh of his own and pivoted to rest his back against the headboard. What a hell of a way to ruin a perfectly wonderful dream, he thought grouchily. If he closed his eyes, he could still picture his dream self. Cool and confident. A cross between Adam Cartwright and Clint Eastwood's character in those spaghetti westerns that made him famous. All charisma and untamed dark energy. A helluva lover. *Better than I ever was with—*

"Stop gloating."

He opened his eyes. He'd been so caught up in the memory he hadn't even heard her open the door. His face went hot, but he denied the charge. "I'm not. I'm…remembering."

"Well, don't," she snapped. "What happened didn't happen. Not really. That wasn't me."

"You were hot."

"Shut up."

"*We* were hot."

"I don't want to talk about it. What happened was a mistake. I've made plenty in my life. All involving the wrong men. I don't even know you well enough to say just how wrong you are, but…never mind. I need to go now. Can you drive? Or should I call my friend to pick me up?"

He looked down. The swollen mass on his chest looked almost normal. A slight puffiness still outlined the black tattoo that encircled his bicep, but the itching had subsided. He shifted around so she could see his back. "I feel okay. How's my neck look? Maybe great sex is a better cure than antihistamines."

Her low growl filled the room, as if from one of her namesake's larger relatives. Puma. Cougar. Angry lioness. "Then get dressed, because we're leaving."

She marched toward the door, chin high, but he could tell she was blinking back tears. "I'll wait outside. And I need to use your phone again," she said, snatching the cell from the table where she'd set it the night before.

"But I'm starving," he said, getting up. The bulk of his clothes were right where he'd left them, neatly draped over the chair in the corner. He pulled on his pants. Strange how his clothing had felt different when he'd been Mad Jack. "Can we at least eat breakfast, first, then I take you home?"

She fumbled with the safety lock.

"I'll meet you at the bike," she said, opening the door. She glanced at her watch. "Tag's dad is going to have my head if he tries to drop off Tag early and I'm not there."

She was out the door before he could ask her why the guy thought he had the right to drop off their kid outside the set times. Jack finished dressing and used the bathroom. He would have liked a shower, but that was going to have to wait. Besides, he wasn't in any hurry for his tattoos to wear off. They were a reminder of the best night of his life. If not for them, he probably never would have been in the same room with Kat, let alone the same bed.

KAT FOUND a shady spot within eyeshot of the motorcycle that reminded her all too vividly of the coal-black horse that Mad Jack had ridden in her dream. She groaned softly and fought back tears. Not only was she a loose woman of questionable morals, she was losing her mind. She needed help. And there was only one person she dared call. Libby.

After a deep breath to steady her hand, she flipped open the phone and punched in the number, remembering too late that there was a time difference between the Hills and the West Coast.

"Hello?"

"Lib? Did I wake you?"

"Kat? No, I'm up. Jenna and I have started taking early-morning walks along the beach. She spent the night with Shane, though, so I'm alone. Coop insists I carry my phone when I go out. I figured this was him checking up on me. He worries like an old woman."

Kat smiled for the first time in what seemed like several centuries. "He loves you, Lib. It's good to worry when you love someone."

"I know. I tease him about it, but actually he's so sweet I can hardly believe this life of mine is real."

Kat was envious. It was natural to kindle a little flame of hope when you witnessed love of this kind in some-one else's life. For a while there, Kat had even dared hope that that kind of love would happen to her. But, no. Instead, she'd spent the night with a client and wound up making love to a figment of her dream—only for real, too.

"Is something wrong, Kat?"

Kat wasn't sure where to begin…or if she should mention the dream part. Would everyone think she was crazy? Maybe she was. "I gave a guy a couple of tattoos and he wound up having an allergic reaction."

"To henna? Is he suing you?"

"No. Not exactly. He provided the ink… That's not why I'm calling. Before his body started swelling like a puffer fish, he'd asked me to show him around the Hills. A paid guide. I said sure. I never turn down a chance to make money, right? But when we got to Custer, he started to go into anaphylactic shock and had to see a doctor. Because of the shot the doctor gave him, he couldn't drive. We had to get a motel room." She paused. "The town is packed. There was only one room left."

Libby giggled. "This story is starting to sound familiar. Was it in a stable?"

Kat let out a small wail. "Not exactly. And there weren't any angels or drummer boys, but…I suppose there could be a baby," she said very, very softly.

Libby was quiet so long Kat wasn't sure she'd heard her strange confession. Then, her voice filled with gravity, she said, "You must have had a good reason to sleep with him. I'm going to assume he's a really great guy and you've fallen in love with him."

"Nice try, Lib, but I don't even know him. He seems okay. Safe. Nice. But I didn't mean to sleep with him. And I didn't. Not exactly. Not *him* him."

"I'm not sure I understand."

"It's complicated."

"Try me. I'm sitting down now."

Kat looked around to be certain nobody was close enough to overhear her confession. "The guy I slept with was in my dream. He was a gunslinger back in 1876 or something. I was a schoolteacher. I remember seeing a dead body on the street and I told him he was callous and unfeeling, then the next thing I knew we were ripping each other's clothes off."

"In your dream."

"I thought so. And I can understand why I dreamed this. I was reading a history book about Seth Bullock and I sorta remember dosing off. But I have no idea where this Mad Jack guy came from. I mean, he's nothing like the Jack I tattooed. Nothing."

"Hmm," Libby said in a tone Kat knew well. Her friend wasn't the type to jump to conclusions. "So, in your dream, you made love with Mad Jack."

"Big-time. It was incredible."

Libby coughed. "But when you woke up, the real-life Jack was in bed with you?"

"Exactly."

"Awkward."

"Tell me about it." Kat knew her body. She had no doubt whatsoever that the sex she'd enjoyed in her dream actually took place.

Neither said anything for a minute or so, then Libby groaned. "They didn't have AIDs in the eighteen hundreds, Kat. You have to go get checked right away. And you're the most fertile person I know. At least, tell me you're on the pill."

Kat closed her eyes and looked skyward. "Why would I be on the pill, Lib? I have no social life. I have no time for a social life."

Libby cleared her throat. Kat knew what was coming next. "When you go to the doctor to get checked, ask him for a morning-after pill. There's a small window of opportunity. I can't remember how long. Are you home?"

"Not yet. I'm waiting for… Oh, there he is."

"Mad Jack?"

Kat snorted. "No. The allergic dentist from Denver."

"Well, whatever you do, don't panic and marry the guy. I'll go online and see what I can find out about your options. We'll figure this out, Kat."

"Thanks, Lib. I'm feeling a lot less homicidal—and/or suicidal—than I was earlier. I'll call you when I get home."

She closed the phone and stood. Jack waited beside the bike, helmets in hand. She took hers from him, but didn't put it on. "Maybe we should have breakfast. And talk."

CHAPTER NINE

THE COFFEE SHOP was packed. Jack's bike was just one of a dozen or more parked in a glittery array of chrome and leather on the street. Kat watched him exchange a few polite nods with the other newcomers. He didn't stick out as a R.U.B. quite as much as she'd imagined he would.

Had something changed? Or was it her? Making love with a person probably had that effect. She'd only been with two other men in her life. And she'd only gone to bed with them after the usual rites of courtship, which had involved wine and beer, respectively. Plus, she'd been distracted by their swoo.

She'd been so sure that Jack's swoo was manageable. And he'd been dead to the world last night when she'd checked to see if he was still breathing. But something had gone wrong. And she honestly didn't know what to say to him.

"Got a booth in the corner, hon," the waitress who was seating people told her. "Good timing."

"The food must be great here," Jack said, taking a plastic menu from a rack on the counter. "Judging by all the business."

"Our cook believes in serving big portions. Soaks up a lot of the mornin' after," she replied wryly as Kat and

Jack trailed behind her. "You both look like you could use a splash of this." She filled two thick white mugs from the steaming carafe in her hand without waiting for a confirmation, then turned to leave. "I'll be back in a few."

Kat slid into the side of the booth facing the back of the restaurant. She'd worked the Days of '76 and the bike rally for enough years that people tended to recognize her. Not that she was a celebrity, like Cooper, but she didn't feel like putting on a fake smile if someone greeted her. Jack took the opposite side, although it wasn't as easy for him to slide in, thanks to the straps on his leather chaps.

He pulled one of the cups closer and ripped open two packets of sugar. He glanced at the menu as he stirred his coffee. "I'm going for the number four, I think. How 'bout you?"

I'll take a morning-after pill, please.

Yes. That was definitely the smart thing to do. Just to be safe.

"English muffin. Extra crisp."

He looked at her. "That's it? I'm buying."

"It's not about money." Although it was *always* about money. Most months she barely scraped by. Student loans, grants, a couple of small scholarships, an occasional check from her father when he sold a buffalo or two. The child-support payments her ex-husbands made barely covered food and clothing for her two growing boys. Any sacrifices that were required to make ends meet came on her end. "I'm not hungry."

"Oh. I understand. You're upset. My sister lost thirty pounds during her divorce. She said she just couldn't eat."

Kat smiled. "I was the opposite. I gained weight both times. Food was comfort."

"Then you must have been a toothpick before you got married, because you're perfect now."

She would have corrected him—she was anything but perfect—or explained about the stress of being a single mom with two rambunctious boys. But their waitress returned to take their order.

Kat was reluctantly impressed that Jack got her request right and added two large orange juices. A luxury at her house.

"So, do you want to talk about what happened now or after breakfast?"

Never. "Now, I guess," she said, taking a sip of coffee.

He reached around to his back pocket and produced a handsome leather billfold. Kat could see several credit-card logos that she recognized. The cards were either gold or platinum. There was cash, too. A lot more than she ever carried. But she knew he wasn't trying to impress her because he quickly tucked it away after he found what he was looking for. "Here's my business card," he said, sliding it across the table. "I have a service that knows how to reach me twenty-four/seven."

She studied the high-end, professional design. Treadwell and Associates. "How many associates?" she asked.

"Eight. Wait. Seven. I'm the eighth. We provide a full gamut of dental options for the whole family, from children's dentistry and orthodontia to an oral surgeon and adult cosmetic dentistry. That's my area."

"You don't work on kids."

"No."

He said the word with such finality she had to ask, "Why?"

"My father was a family dentist. Worked alone for

thirty years. Had a thriving practice. Loved helping people so much that he often opened the office on weekends to work on kids who couldn't afford to pay for dental services."

Something in his tone reminded her of the dead look in Mad Jack's eyes when he told her why he gave up on people. "One day, one of his charity kids accused my dad of touching him inappropriately. The politically correct way of saying my dad was a pedophile."

"Oh, my God. What happened?"

"Nothing good. Dad's insurance company talked him into settling on the condition the complaint was dropped. That's not the same as being vindicated in court. Rumors spread. Dad's business fell off. He retired early. And died too young."

Kat could hear his pain. She didn't blame him for not wanting to work on kids. "I'm sorry."

"Me, too. Dad was a great guy. He loved kids. He didn't do what that child said he did. The boy later recanted. Claimed his stepfather coached him and his mother—a drug addict at the time—made him say what he did."

"How horrible for your family."

Jack shrugged. "I still followed in his footsteps. I simply specialized in an area that doesn't require me to deal with children. I'm not good with them. Ask your son."

Kat already knew Tag's opinion of Jack, but she kept it to herself. "I think I heard you say your mother lived near you. Did she remarry after your father passed?"

She pictured her own mother. Now on husband number five. Or was it six?

He fiddled with the empty sugar wrapper. "No. She

had her career to occupy her. Banking. She was a vice president of one of our local banks. She just retired."

Kat slipped his card into her hip pocket. She already had his cell-phone number programmed on her phone at home. Not that there would be any reason to contact him. Not if she did the smart thing.

She realized he'd asked something that she'd missed. "Sorry. What?"

"Since we're strolling down memory lane, I wondered about your childhood. Happy? Messed up? Normal?"

"Normal?"

His eyebrow arched in a way that told her she'd revealed more with one word than she'd intended. "I have no idea what that is. But I'm pretty sure it doesn't involve fighting for custody of a kid you then ignore because of all the other drama in your life."

"Your parents are divorced, I take it."

She took a deep breath and let it out. "Okay. Here's the short version. My mom is a needy person who grasped at any hint of security. My dad is a rancher who likes people to think he's more successful than he is. Mom saw the outward trappings and thought she had it made. Only, by the time I was born she realized she'd made a terrible mistake. Dad abuses alcohol and when you're in the middle of nowhere with two kids from a previous marriage and a tiny baby and a crazy man who tells you you're dirt, your options are limited. She took his pride and joy—a ridiculous boat of a car that my half brother called the pimpmobile—when she left. Dad couldn't very well sic his attorneys on her for custody of the car, so he went after me. They battled for years."

"He must have wanted you in his life."

"He wanted to win. He has this Old West thing about never giving up a square inch of land or a single concession when negotiating with the enemy. He tells everyone my mother made him spend my college fund on lawyer fees."

He cocked his head. "Do you have a relationship with him now?"

"Sorta. I lived with him when I was in high school. Mom was married to a psycho preacher at the time and I didn't have anywhere else to go. Dad pretty much ignored me the whole time, but that was okay because I had my buffalo to keep me occupied."

His cup wobbled as he set it down. "Buffalo?"

"I talked Dad into buying a few head of bison when I was a sophomore. He kept them even after I moved out and got married. The boys and I visit the ranch to check on them every couple of weeks."

"Where's this?"

"Near Belle Fourche. Northern Hills. Lately, Dad's gotten involved in marketing the meat for sale. His half of the herd, not mine. But he keeps my freezer filled, and that's come in pretty handy at times."

She was saved from spilling any more of her guts by the arrival of their food. As promised, Jack's platter-size plate was heaped with three eggs, hash-brown potatoes and a slab of ham half an inch thick.

Her muffin looked silly by comparison.

Their waitress slapped down a bottle of ketchup, a little container of hot sauce and a plastic tub filled with various flavors of jelly without being asked. "Enjoy," she said. "Holler if you need more juice."

They ate in silence for a few minutes. Jack had very nice manners, she noticed. He chewed with his mouth closed. Something she was constantly harping on with Tag. Of course, part of his problem was that eye tooth, which was coming in sideways.

"So, is it safe to say you and your dad aren't close?" Jack asked after washing down a bite with a gulp of juice.

She nibbled on her muffin but couldn't work up an appetite. "I wanted us to be when I was a little girl. Now we mostly talk about the herd when we see each other. I tried living with him another time, too. When Tag was a baby and Pete and I first broke up. It didn't last long. Dad wanted a live-in maid, and I wanted a father who gave a damn."

"What happened?"

She sighed. "I convinced Pete that my milk was going to dry up and he'd have to pay for formula if he didn't help me rent an apartment in town. I was just getting back on my feet when I met ex number two." She snickered softly. "They say mistakes aren't mistakes if you learn from them, right? I learned that nursing is not a surefire form of contraception."

He laughed. "That's wisdom for you—arriving too late to be of any help when you need it most. So where's your mom live?"

"Spearfish. Her last husband moved out a week after she was diagnosed with throat cancer. Poor Mom. She always believed she was getting a guy to take care of her, but it never worked out that way. Fortunately her sister, my aunt Roberta, was available to move in. Her doctors claim to have the cancer in remission, but now

Mom's dealing with depression. I think she's worried that no man is ever going to love her again."

She shook her head. "This is really unpleasant conversation for breakfast. I'm sorry."

He shrugged. "Don't apologize. I asked."

"So what about you? Are you close to your mom?"

"More so when I was engaged to a woman she thought was perfect for me. Actually, I think Mom took our breakup harder than either Jaydene or I did."

His eyes glinted with a roguish look that reminded her of the man in her dream. Her heartbeat sped up, despite her attempt to ignore the little thrill that shot through her body.

Okay. So she wished Jack was her dream lover in real life. But he wasn't. And she wasn't a virginal schoolmarm, either. *Forget about Mad Jack.*

"What was that?" he asked.

Had she muttered that out loud? Oh, dear. She really was losing it. "Nothing. I guess I should be grateful my parents are utterly self-absorbed. I don't take advice that well. My mother used to call me 'sweetly stubborn.'"

Jack refilled both their cups from the insulated carafe their waitress had left behind, then he eased back in the booth. His tattoos were still a little tender, but thankfully the itching had subsided.

He watched her nibble on a piece of muffin she'd topped with grape jelly. He found the gesture childlike. And a fist—solid and unfamiliar—wrapped around his heart and squeezed. He might have feared that the chicken-fried steak from a few nights earlier had already clogged his arteries, but his subconscious mind told him that wasn't the case. He liked this woman. A lot. Even if she wasn't her dream alter ego. Katherine. Who was much better suited to him. After all, the schoolmarm's children went home to their own families each night. Kat's didn't.

"Are you done?" she asked, consulting her watch. "I should be going."

"In case your ex-husband brings your son home early."

"Partly. And by the way, I don't go out of my way to accommodate Pete. I do it for Tag. Because he has enough drama in his life from his stepmom and half siblings without watching his parents' power struggles."

That made sense. In a way. And normally he would let the statement go unchallenged. But instead, he asked, "Aren't you afraid that you might be sending the wrong message?"

"Pardon?"

"Well, you're a strong woman, and catering to your ex-husband's whims might make your son think that's what women do."

Her eyes narrowed. "Armchair parenting again."

"Huh?"

"Call me when you're a father and we'll ta—" She stopped abruptly and didn't finish the sentence.

He wanted to ask why, but suddenly he understood. They'd had unprotected sex. She could be pregnant. With his child. The food he'd devoured shifted uncomfortably in his belly.

"You're not… You don't think…"

Her cheeks turned rosy pink and she wouldn't meet his eyes. "I don't know," she said, making a show of folding her paper napkin. "But my friend reminded me that there's a pill I can take that wasn't readily available when I got pregnant with my sons."

He'd heard of it. "I thought it was only prescribed in Europe."

She shook her head. "Apparently not."

Jack picked up the bill their waitress had deposited on the table a few minutes earlier and stood. His mind was jumping all over the place and he really couldn't think.

Did he approve of her plan? Sure. Of course. He must. Because the alternative was so not in the realm of possibility it didn't even bear scrutiny. Right?

Once they were outside and preparing to get aboard his bike, he asked, "Just out of curiosity, would you have used that pill if it had been available when you became pregnant with your sons?"

Her frown intensified. "That's not a fair question. At the time I might have welcomed the option, but I can't imagine my life without my boys. Tag and Jordie are the best thing that ever happened to me."

He believed her. She was a natural-born mother. His mother was not. "But considering the circumstances—getting pregnant out of wedlock—surely the thought of having an abor—"

She cut him off. "Not my thing. And I was married to both their father's before either of my sons were born."

The flinty look in her eye reminded him of Katherine. She stood her ground, too, when it mattered. "Got it. Like I said, I was just curious. Shall we go?"

She nodded, then pulled on her helmet.

Seconds later, they were on the road headed back toward the heart of the Black Hills. Jack looked around with a funny sense of disorientation. Nothing looked familiar. Probably because he'd been suffering from an allergic reaction when they first pulled into town. Either that, or he still had one foot in another time.

CHAPTER TEN

"SO WHAT DID HE DO? Just drop you off at your door and drive away? That doesn't sound very heroic," Jenna complained.

Jenna had been so busy since her return dealing with the Mystery Spot and trying to prepare for the filming that was scheduled to begin next week that Kat hadn't had much chance to talk to her. This was the first Jenna had heard about Kat's close encounter with the dentist from Denver.

Thanks to blabbermouth Char.

"Well, she couldn't very well ask him in when Pete and Tag were sitting in the driveway when Kat and the R.U.B. pulled in, could she?" Char asked.

"What were they doing there? I thought Pete had planned to keep Tag all weekend."

So had Kat. But thanks to her damnable luck—and Pete's demanding new wife—he'd been forced to cut short his camping trip. "Michelle didn't think it was fair to Aiden to miss out on all the fun, so she planned a family day on Sunday. Naturally that didn't include Tag," Kat said, frowning.

"Could have been worse. Jordie's dad could have brought him back early, too," Char said.

Kat looked at Libby for help.

Char was a dear friend, but men were immediately suspect in her book until they proved themselves worthy. And since Libby—mother confessor of them all—had been in California at the time of this fiasco, Kat had turned to Char for help in deciding what to do about Jack.

To Kat's chagrin, Char insisted on calling Jack "The R.U.B.," even though she knew his name.

"The fact that Jack played along and didn't blow her cover makes him somewhat heroic, doesn't it?" Libby asked. "He could have pulled out an imaginary six-gun and started a real showdown."

Jenna and Char looked at each other as though completely lost. "He carries a gun?"

"Isn't that against the law?"

Kat knew it was time to get the Wine, Women and Words book club back on track. She reached for the talking stick—a gnarled, venerable limb that had been with them since the beginning—and rapped it on the floor. The talking stick secured the speaker's right to be heard without interruption. Unfortunately the sound was muffled by old shag carpeting, but the motion caught everyone's attention.

"About the book—didn't you all love it?"

Libby nodded with enthusiasm. "I was particularly impressed by how the author was able to pass back and forth between two times—the past and the present—with such fluidity."

Kat shot her a warning look. There were elements about that night with Jack that she hadn't told anyone else. Her dream. Mad Jack. The only reason she'd told Libby on the phone that morning was because it had seemed so surreal and she'd been desperate to make sense of what happened. But that didn't mean she planned to share news of her mental instability with the other members of their group.

During the ten days that had passed since that fateful night, Kat had given a lot of thought to what transpired—and why. She'd finally decided someone must have slipped a couple of hallucinatory mushrooms on her pizza. That was the only reasonable explanation.

Libby didn't agree. She believed in things like fate and destiny, soul mates and love that could transcend time. The stuff of fiction, in other words, Kat thought with justifiable bitterness, taking a sip of the sparkling grape juice Char had brought, instead of wine.

Libby was the only pregnant one among them, but the other three had agreed to forgo alcohol at tonight's meeting.

At least, Kat hoped Libby was the only pregnant one among them. She couldn't swear to the fact because when it had come time to make that monumental decision regarding the morning-after pill, her decision-making ability stalled. Thanks to Tag and Jordie.

She'd peeked into Tag's bedroom one night and discovered Jordie curled up beside his brother. He'd been sneaking into Tag's room in the middle of the night ever since they moved into this three-bedroom house. Kat was waiting for Tag to throw a fit and demand his privacy, but he never did.

The thought had occurred to her for the first time that maybe the two brothers traveled together in their dreams.

For a good hour images of their childhood had flashed before her eyes and she'd known without a doubt that being their mother had been her destiny—even if a happily-ever-after with the love of her life was not so preordained.

If fate or the swoo or a bad mushroom had tricked her into screwing up again, so be it, she'd decided the next morning. She'd deal with the consequences when the time came. Just like she had the times before.

"You know, Kat's R.U.B. is still around," Char said out of the blue, and so far from the subject of the book that Kat squawked and pointed the talking stick at her. "Well, it's true," Char said, defending her point.

"But not relevant."

"Interesting, though," Jenna said, her pretty red pony-tail whipping back and forth as she looked from Char to Kat. "I thought you said the biker-dude dentist was headed back to Denver, Kat."

According to the last of the dozen or so messages Jack had left on her phone two days ago, she could reach him by cell "…if the need arose." She hadn't returned any of his calls because…well, she knew how this game ended, so why bother with the middle innings?

He hadn't specifically said he was leaving town, but his tone had held a certain resignation, which she'd assumed meant he'd given up on her neurotic behavior and had returned home. "Um…I've been running every which way this week getting things organized for the rally. I still can't believe I forgot to turn in my vendor application," she said wearily, softly knocking the talking stick against her brow. "Now, I'm going to have to find a way to farm out the boys, because there isn't any room for me on Main Street and they're much too young to see what goes on in Thunder Alley."

Thunder Alley was the name of a popular campground a few miles from downtown Sturgis. For a week every August, the flat, mostly treeless field became a bustling city filled with thousands of people doing pretty much exactly what they wanted.

"Are you sure you want to do that, Kat?" Jenna asked. "You'll make twice as much as an extra once filming starts."

"I know. I talked to Shane this morning. He told me he's not going to need the extras until the middle of next week, so I should be able to do both." Shane Reynard was both the director/producer of the television show and Jenna's unofficial fiancé. "Unlike Libby and Coop, we're not in a huge rush to tie the knot," she'd explained when she first arrived at Kat's house. "We're quite content to live in exquisite sin."

Kat was happy—really happy—for her friend, and Jenna's determined effort to see that Kat was hired as an extra couldn't have come at a better time—except where child care was concerned.

"Normally I could switch weeks with Pete, but he and Michelle are flying back East to visit Michelle's parents."

"And let me guess," Char said. "They're not taking Tag."

Kat shook her head. "Pete claims it's because he has to return early for work. Can you imagine how miserable Tag would be? Alone with Michelle and the kids?" She could.

"And Drew's on the road this week. I know because he was late with his check and his wife gave me this big sob story about cutbacks and the price of gas— Never mind. You've heard this story before." She held up the dog-eared copy of the trade paperback she'd gotten at the library. "Speaking of stories, didn't the author do a marvelous job of making you feel what it would be like to be old? I felt a lot more sympathy for the things my mother has been going through. I know she's not that old, but cancer can really age a person."

Libby took the talking stick from Kat. "I cried every time we were in the old man's point of view. I felt so sorry for him—locked in a body that wouldn't cooperate. Reduced to a person no one listened to or respected. I thought he and my grandmother would have been good friends if they'd known each other."

Mention of Mary—Libby's grandmother who had practically raised Libby and her brother, Mac—caused a temporary sidetrack of conversation. Kat was sorry to learn that the lovely old woman seemed to be declining faster than anyone could handle—especially Lib.

"At least she lived her life with style and grace for nearly every one of her ninety-plus years," Jenna insisted. "My mother will be the first to tell you she wasted way too much time worrying about what my father thought, instead of following her dreams. I can honestly say I've never seen Mom happier or more alive than she is now. Have you seen her yet? The transformation is amazing. And she truly owns the part she plays on the show. It's exciting."

Kat listened to this new topic for a few minutes before taking back the talking stick. "I can't wait to see your mom in action, Jenna, but I have a couple more study questions about the book to bring up. The person who hosts is supposed to think up six, right?"

Char groaned. "You take everything so literally."

Kat ignored her. "Did anyone else think the ending was unrealistic?"

"Me," Char said with feeling. "Nobody would saddle himself with that kind of responsibility on a whim."

"I thought the circus owner was kind and compassionate," Jenna said. "He respected the past. Think of the stories the old man could tell."

"Until he broke a hip or dementia set in and he couldn't remember his name," Libby put in.

The defeat in Lib's voice told Kat that Grandma Mary was worse off than any of them knew.

"Taking care of an old person can be as draining as caring for an infant," she went on. "In some ways, it's worse because you don't expect any help from a baby, but a part of you can't let go of how that person used to be."

Kat's grip on the talking stick slipped. Any mention of the word *baby* made her nervous. She felt fine. No early-warning nipple tenderness like when she was first pregnant with her boys, but she wouldn't feel completely out of the woods until her period started—in another day or two.

Char caught the stick with one hand, but the look she gave Kat seemed particularly intense. "You're kinda spacey tonight, Kat," Char said. "Are you okay?"

"Sure. Fine. Like I said, it was a crazy week. And that whole thing with the R.U.B.…I mean, Jack…well…" She cleared her throat. "Who's ready for dessert? Since the story was about a circus, I bought Cracker Jacks, ice cream and all the toppings for sundaes, and two flavors of cotton candy—turquoise and hot pink." She made a face. "Those are the colors. I have no idea what flavor either is supposed to represent. Can you believe they sell it pre-spun in a bag? That's just wrong, isn't it?"

She'd stood up and was halfway to the kitchen when she realized nobody else had moved. She pivoted on one heel and followed the group's collective gaze toward the door—where a man was standing at the closed screen. His hand lifted to knock.

"Um, hello," he said. "Sorry to interrupt. I saw the extra cars in the driveway, but your son said they belonged to the neighbor and it was okay to come up."

Kat had sent the boys out front to play catch. Apparently they'd decided to play a trick probably meant to embarrass both Kat and Jack.

Char jumped to her feet. "Hey, I remember you. We met on the street, and someone matching your description bought a couple of nice pieces of jewelry from my shop yesterday while I was in town at the bank."

Jack stepped closer to the screen but didn't open it. "Right. Kat pointed out your very unique store when we passed it. I didn't see you. Was there a video camera?"

She laughed in a very un-Char-like way. "Better. Pia, my clerk, is into men. Believe me, if you'd been wearing a skirt, she wouldn't have been able to tell me squat. But in your case I got a full description. Right down to your boots and the color of your motorcycle."

Kat looked for support from Libby, who smiled benignly. Either pregnancy had robbed her of any desire to meddle in her friends' lives or she was still thinking about her grandmother. Jenna's gaze seemed to take in every detail of the moment—the writer in her obviously intrigued.

All three women looked at Kat expectantly. She

could tell they felt she should invite him in. Stifling a sigh, she changed directions. Opening the door, she motioned him inside. "I figured from your phone message you were back in Denver."

"Really? Which one of the dozen or so led you to think that?" he asked just loud enough for her to hear.

Kat's cheeks turned uncomfortably hot.

He let her off the hook before she could come up with a plausible lie…excuse. "I lucked out. My hotel had a cancelation, so I was able to extend my stay until today. I planned to be on the road this morning. But after talking to Brian last night, I decided it was kind of silly to buy a bike and come all this way without sticking around for at least a few days of the Sturgis Rally. He said I couldn't get a true sense of the wild and woolly Old West until I hung out in Thunder Alley." He shook his head and said to the other women, "I'm a total sucker for history."

"Thunder Alley!" Kat exclaimed, forgetting about their audience. "I thought you didn't like crowds."

His gray eyes were inscrutable. Dressed all in black, he resembled his dream counterpart more than he could possibly know. "All part of the experience," he said with a shrug of the shoulder she'd tattooed. She couldn't see it because he was wearing a lightweight button-up shirt. "I have more vacation time saved up than I know what to do with, so since I'm here, I figured I might as well give it a try."

"Were you able to get a room?" Char asked, drawing Jack's gaze away from Kat's. "Hotels are usually booked solid months in advance."

"So I found out. Brian offered to rent me a room at his place for a grand, but his wife wasn't exactly thrilled.

He tracked me down today to tell me she kicked him out. Filed for divorce. And changed the locks on the door."

Kat winced. She looked over her shoulder and told the others, "He's talking about Brian Whitlock. Lives in Nemo. I can't remember his wife's name. They have three little kids. The youngest is Jordie's age. They were in T-ball together." But a part of her mind hadn't let go of the words *a grand*. He was seriously considering spending a thousand dollars for a place to sleep for a week?

With an extra grand in the bank, she wouldn't have to work at the bar part-time while she was student-teaching.

As if reading her thoughts, Jack said, "I stopped by to see if you know anybody who might have a spare room to rent."

She made a split-second decision. Not unlike the circus owner in the book they were just talking about. Jack needed a place to stay. She needed money. Her boys could bunk together, and it wasn't as if she was going to sleep with Jack again. That was a one-night aberration. *Maybe if he were Mad Jack...* She shook her head. "No. I mean, yes. I mean, you could stay here. In Jordie's room. He and Tag can share a room."

He didn't jump at the offer, and for a few stomach-sickening seconds Kat felt the same way she had when the parent who was supposed to pick her up on exchange day didn't show. She felt unwanted.

"Um...I appreciate the offer," he said hesitantly. "But I think you better run that by your sons first. The older one and I got off on the wrong foot. The little guy seemed pretty friendly until...Tag, right?...elbowed him. I don't think they'd be too happy to have me bunking here all week."

Kat could picture what he described. Tag called the shots and Jordie went along with whatever his big brother wanted.

"Tough. They're not paying the rent. I'm the grown-up. I get to make this call."

Libby cleared her throat and sat forward, her hands pressed together in her lap. "Um…Kat, this is none of my business, but I can't picture Pete being okay with you letting a stranger sleep across the hall from his son." To Jack, she said apologetically, "That's not to imply anything about you, but Pete's as suspicious as they come."

Damn. Leave it to Lib to state the obvious. Kat didn't have the slightest doubt about Jack and she knew with every ounce of conviction in her soul that he would never be a threat to her boys. If anything, they intimidated him. He even believed them when they said she was home alone.

But Pete was another story. When he found out, there would be hell to pay. Maybe another trip to the custody mediator. She couldn't put Tag through that again. Nor could she afford it.

With a sigh, she looked at Jack and said, "Unfortunately Libby's right. I was seeing a positive balance in my checkbook when I start student-teaching, but Tag's dad would definitely throw a hissy." She tossed up her hands. "But I'd be happy to ask around. In fact, Lib, maybe he could rent Gran's old cabin."

Libby shook her head. "The film crew has nailed down every spare bed in Sentinel Pass. And most couches, too. I told Coop the timing sucked, but they didn't have any choice."

Kat shrugged. "I guess you could look in Rapid. I doubt if Spearfish would have anything. Maybe Custer."

The name Custer made Jack look at her.

"I have an idea," Char said, springing to her feet. "Let me ponder this while I help Kat serve dessert. Jack, have a chair while Libby and Jenna grill you… I mean, entertain you. Come on, pal," she said, taking Kat's elbow. "I'll help make the sundaes."

Char hustled her into the kitchen with barely a backward glance. Jack had dropped into her chair and kicked out his feet as if he were home. The weird part was he didn't look out of place. She didn't know how that was possible.

Char snapped her fingers in front of Kat's face. "Girl, this is not like you. Goddamn. The swoo has taken your brain and replaced it with a sea sponge."

Kat made a face. "Shh. He'll hear you. This is a small house," she said in a low whisper. "Get the ice-cream bowls out of the freezer and put them on that tray. Everything is all ready to go."

She reached into the overhead cupboard for the ridiculously overpriced parcels of gossamer sugar. She'd had to hide them behind the tinned vegetables to keep the boys from pilfering.

"What are you thinking?" she asked, stretching to locate the last bag.

"That you have it bad for that guy."

Her hand brushed against a can of peas and she had to do a quick impersonation of a juggler to keep everything from falling out. Once the last can was back in place, she turned and faced Char. Hands on hips, she barked, "I do not."

The volume of her protest seemed to echo in the small room. The room where she'd sat with her nose mere inches from Jack Treadwell's perfectly shaped pectoral muscles.

She scowled at Char and returned to the very important job of setting out the cotton candy in an artful manner. "I need the money, Char. Next semester is going to be tough because I won't have as much time at night and after classes to work. That's the only reason I agreed to set up my tent in the campground. You know how crappy that area can be for a woman alone. The last time I worked there Pete was with me. Nobody gave me any grief because...well, Pete is Pete. But this year..."

"That's part of my plan, swoo girl," Char said, setting down the tray she'd carried from the freezer. She rubbed her hands together. Whether from the cold or in expectation, Kat couldn't say.

"Huh?" She picked up the two extra packages of spun sugar and debated what to do with them. She'd planned to give them to her boys as a reward for behaving while her friends were here. But after that stunt with Jack...

Char's voice cut into her brooding. "...I take Jordie for the week? He and I got along great while we were at the powwow. I have to be on the road a couple of days, but I always stay with friends who have kids, so he'd be more than welcome. And I could use the extra help on the weekend at the tepee."

"Really?" The offer was unexpected, and generous. "He'd love that. What an adventure. But honestly, Char, I didn't think you were...well, that into kids."

Char's lips pursed in a kind of introspective way. "They're a fact of life, and I like yours just fine."

"I'm glad. But Jordie's dad isn't the problem. He doesn't really care what I do as long as it doesn't cost him more child support." She hated to say the words out loud because she never wanted Jordie to think his father didn't love him. Drew did love his son; he simply loved whatever was going on in his life at the moment more.

"I know. And believe me, Jordie does, too. And he's okay with his dad's shortcomings. You've more than made up for them by being a super-cool mom."

"Really?" The warm feeling in her midsection was cut short by Jenna's voice calling from the other room.

"Are you churning that ice cream by hand or did you have to milk the cow first?"

Char growled. "We're coming. How do you stay so slim when you eat like a horse?"

Jenna whinnied in response.

Char added spoons to the tray and started to leave, but Kat stopped her. "I really appreciate you offering to keep Jordie, but what will I do with Tag? I suppose I could call my dad, but…"

Char motioned with her head, which as usual sported unusual highlights. Tonight's were maroon. "I have a plan for him, too. I just wanted to see if you were cool with me taking Jordie."

"Why wouldn't I be? He hasn't stopped talking about the powwow since he got back. He says you rock."

Char beamed, but she kept walking. "Okay, you voracious dessert eaters. Did you explain to the R.U.B. about the book and why we're eating enough sugar in one sitting to induce a diabetic coma in a person who doesn't have the disease?"

Everybody chuckled, but that didn't prevent them

from digging in. Jack, too, since Kat gave him her portion. Her stomach was too upset to digest anything. "Actually, Char," Jack said, using his spoon for emphasis, "I read *Water for Elephants* when it first hit the *New York Times'* list. My then girlfriend was on a reading kick and insisted that we read the same books so we could discuss them."

The women all exchanged a look that even Jack could interpret. He tossed his head and laughed. "Yeah, I know. That makes me a real wuss, doesn't it? But to be fair, I got to pick every other title. And we wound up reading some good books. Personally I loved this one, although I had issues with the ending."

Libby looked at Kat and gave a little nod Kat hoped nobody else saw. She picked up a box with a familiar logo and carefully opened it to withdraw a kernel of caramel popcorn. She drew it closer and poked around with her finger. *Do they still put prizes inside?* She didn't know.

"Kat?"

She looked up. Oh, God. Somehow she'd tuned out the conversation that had been going on around her. "Um…yes?"

Jenna checked with the others first, then said, "Char suggested that I take Tag home with me. Mom and her friend, Rollie, won't be coming for a few days. Tag could have her bed until they get here, then there's always the couch."

"But you're busy at the Mystery Spot. Didn't you say you're shorthanded at the moment?"

"Yes. That's the point. Remember when we talked about him *working* for me this summer?" She said the word in a way that reminded Kat that the previously discussed job—the same one she and Jack had argued about—was more about keeping Tag busy and feeling useful than actually earning a living.

"But without your more experienced people there, Tag might be a nuisance."

Jenna shook her head. "I don't think so. I was about his age when I started helping out. There are plenty of things for him to do—even just picking up trash. I promise I won't overwork him. He'll have fun, too."

Kat wasn't sure what to say.

"Um…wasn't your reason for Tag not working at the Mystery Spot the cost of gas it would take to drive him there?" Jack asked.

Kat sensed her friends' surprise that she'd discussed her son's job—or lack of one—with Jack. "Yes," she said shortly.

"Well, I have to cover for my manager all week," Jenna said, her tone triumphant. "If he's staying with me, then it wouldn't cost you anything. We'll bike there and back together. So?" She eyed Kat. "Can he come home with me?"

Kat wanted to say yes. Knowing the boys were safe and having fun with people who wanted to spend time with them would free her to work as long and as hard as she could stand it. And no child-care bill would mean more money in the bank this fall. "Are you two sure you know what you're getting into? We're talking boisterous little boys. They're not sweet and docile like Megan."

"My four-and-a-half-year-old niece," Libby explained to Jack. "She's an angel. For everyone, except her father, who she has wrapped around her finger."

"Oh," Jack said.

His tone was polite, but uninterested. Kat could tell he wanted to hear her decision.

"Just promise me," she said, "you're not doing this because you feel sorry for me."

Libby shook her head. "We're trying to help out, you goof. That's what friends do. With both kids out of the house, you could rent Jordie's room *and* Tag's, if you were so inclined."

"Maybe Brian needs a place," Char said with a loud raspberry tacked on for good measure.

Everyone laughed, but Jack set the record straight. "Brian moved in with his mother. I suggested he give AA a try, but that didn't go over so great."

Kat could imagine. Her dad had blown up at any insinuation that he had a problem with alcohol. She'd heard from several sources—including Buck himself—that he'd stopped drinking, but Kat wasn't holding her breath. Besides, even if Dad was reformed now, the damage his drinking had inflicted on others continued to haunt all of his children, including Kat.

"Brian's a nice guy. This might be the wake-up call he needs to get his life back on track. I'll try to bring up the subject with him the next time I'm working at Pop's. Which won't be until *after* the rally," Kat said pointedly. "So it looks like I have a room to rent, Jack. Do we have a deal? A thousand dollars for a bed and private bath. Tonight through, say, Sunday morning? We have Coop's big party in Sentinel Pass on Sunday afternoon, right, Lib? I could pick up the boys there."

Jack set his dish aside and put out his hand to shake.

Kat braced herself for his touch. She'd been thinking

about his hands and the yummy sensations they'd created in her body far too often since that night. To her surprise, he kept the contact short and sweet, businesslike. She stepped back just the same. Even a little residual swoo would not go unnoticed by her observant friends.

She glanced at Jenna first, then Char. "If you're sure about this, I'll go talk to the boys."

Jenna and Char looked at each other a moment before scrambling to their feet. "Let us," Jenna said.

Char nodded. "If they don't want to come, I don't want you to pressure them into it. Not that you would, exactly, but you know how you try to make everybody happy and well…never mind. Give us five minutes."

"Ten," Jenna corrected. "Tag and I have to negotiate his *salary*," she added with a wink.

They disappeared out the door before Kat could decide if she'd been insulted or not. She glanced at Libby, who was staring with an amused, proud-mother look on her face—even though her body was barely showing the baby bump the gossip magazines had been speculating about.

"I can understand why Jenna's so enthused about spending time with Tag," she said conversationally. "From the moment she saw those Burnese mountain dog puppies, she's had motherhood on the brain. But what's up with Char? I didn't think she had a maternal bone in her body."

Kat couldn't say. In fact, Char had resisted Kat's initial plea to babysit Jordie that fateful Wednesday when she'd subbed for Becky at Pop's. Something must have happened that made the boy less of a previously assumed pain in the butt.

Kat wasn't too worried about how her sons would behave. They were well mannered and polite and they ate with their mouths closed—most of the time. She was proud of them and confident they could be trusted to play in grown-up sandboxes when required. They'd be fine.

She only hoped she could say the same for herself. She'd agreed to spend six nights under the same roof with a man who'd somehow managed to nail her without a single drop of booze passing between her lips. Whatever kind of swoo Jack possessed, it was unlike any she'd known before. *And* it seemed to bridge two worlds—the present and the past.

That fact alone should have scared the hell out of her, but it was too late to back out now. The boys would regard this opportunity to stay with Char and Jenna as a mini-vacation. The only kind Kat could afford. Especially if her period failed to show up on time.

She could handle Jack and his time-traveling swoo, she told herself firmly. He was here. And now. And that was how they both were going to stay.

CHAPTER ELEVEN

"ARE YOU SURE about this? I could probably buy camping gear and set up a tent."

He was helping her change the sheets on her son's bed half an hour or so after the ball that he'd inadvertently set in motion took off like a rocket. Those book-club women really got things done, he silently acknowledged.

"It's fine," Kat mumbled, giving the top sheet a crisp snap. Jack inhaled fresh air and sunshine, not the artificial perfume of a dryer sheet. "I fold and tuck the corners," she told him.

He knew how to make a bed, but he didn't argue. Instead, he did as asked, and continued to look around the room. It felt on the small side and was definitely decorated in the eclectic clutter of a young boy, but he couldn't spot a speck of dust on the shelves above the desk, and there was no lingering odor of sweat socks that he remembered from being in an all-male dorm in college.

"Didn't I hear you tell Tag that you never went camping?" She was already done with her side and waited with the lightweight cotton blanket balled against her chest. Her eyes had that challenging twinkle he'd noticed the night they met.

"That's true, but there's a first time for everything, right? And I'd give it a try if this was too uncomfortable for you."

Something in her expression changed. Softened. She gave him the same indulgent smile she'd used with her son that afternoon of the tattoo. He got the impression she'd forgive his shortcomings as long as he was honest about them. Why? Because the men in her life were never truthful? Or were they just never up-front about their flaws?

"I appreciate the gesture, but this probably isn't the best venue to try out a new skill. I can tell you from experience that the campgrounds are wall-to-wall tents and bodies. And if you don't have the right equipment, the mosquitoes will eat you alive."

She plumped a pillow, then picked up a matching blue-and-white-stripe pillowcase. Wedging one end under her chin, she added, "By the way, how are your tattoos?"

He yanked the collar of his recently laundered T-shirt down and to the left, exposing the slightly withered-looking outline of his favorite tattoo. "Almost gone. Truthfully, I'm really sorry I didn't listen to you in the first place. I remember those pictures you showed me of how henna slowly fades. I would have preferred that. Plus, we might have skipped a trip to the emergency room."

The pillow plunked to the bed. The pillowcase hung limply in her hand. Her mouth was open wide enough for him to see four fillings in her molars. Other than those, her teeth were perfect. "Wait a minute. Did you just admit that you were wrong and I was right?"

He nodded slowly. Was that a trick question? "Yes. I should have listened to you. You're the expert. I was paying for your expertise. I tell people that all the time in my business. But some patients—people like me, apparently—come into the office with one thing in mind and can't be dissuaded. You did your best to talk me into a better choice, and we both know I was wrong."

Her cheeks flashed with color and she quickly resumed her task. With a tender pat, she smoothed the striped bedspread and stepped back. "There you go. I hope you'll be comfortable. The mattress isn't extra long, you can stretch out at an angle."

He'd noticed the clever conformation of the bunk bed the first time he'd visited the house. Instead of the double-decker model he remembered from his first year in the dorm, this unit sported a double bed on the bottom and perpendicular to it, creating an L-shape, was the upper twin, with a ladder built in to the end support.

"I'll be fine," he said. "With the pillow on that end, you get a sort of cavelike effect. I like that. Butch Cassidy and the Sundance Kid holed up in a cave with their gang. I always thought that sounded kind of adventurous."

She bent over to gather up the dirty sheets. As she did, she explained the rationale behind the bed purchase. "Before we moved in here, we lived in a two-bedroom apartment. I gave the boys the bigger room and I slept on a futon beside my desk so I could study at night. But when my mom got sick, it looked as though I might wind up taking care of her, so I went hunting for a bigger place. Since this bed can accommodate three, I figured I could give her my bed, move Jordie in here—

he sneaks in most nights, anyway, then if we had company, I could take the top bunk."

"You're awfully quick to give up your bed," he said casually.

Her shoulders stiffened. "What's that supposed to mean? Listen, I thought we established that I'm not easy and I don't usually jump in bed with—"

He held up both hands. "Whoa. Not what I meant. You're generous. You put other people's needs ahead of your own. I wasn't putting you down."

"Oh."

"But since you brought up the subject, is it okay to ask what you decided? I thought you might call and let me know. About the morning-after pill, I mean."

She hugged the bundle in her arms tighter and rested her chin on the fabric with a sigh. She worked the corner of her mouth—the mouth he'd been fantasizing about for days—with her bottom teeth for a few seconds before answering. "I should have called. I'm sorry. But I figured if you didn't hear from me, you'd assume no news was good news."

Her blasé tone didn't gibe with the serious look in her eyes. But she changed the subject before he could pin down her answer to something more concrete.

"I better toss these in the laundry basket and go over my checklist for tomorrow. A new venue means new challenges," she said with an air of resignation. She glanced around once, then left the room.

There would be time, he told himself. As he'd gathered from her very friendly friends, Kat was setting up a tattoo booth in the wild and woolly campgrounds he'd heard so much about. In fact, Libby, the auburn-hair

beauty to whom the others seemed to differ, had pulled
him aside while Kat was helping her sons pack.

"Kat won't ask for help, Jack, but we're all worried
about her working the tattoo booth inside the campground. I've always heard anything goes in Thunder
Alley. Normally I wouldn't have pushed the idea of a
relative stranger moving in, but you seem pretty decent.
I'll sleep better knowing you have her back."

He could have sworn he detected a slight emphasis
on the word *sleep*. Had Kat shared with her friends the
fact that she'd spent the night in his bed?

He followed her through the spotless kitchen. Jack
had offered to help Libby clean up once Kat had joined
Jenna and Char in the driveway with the boys, but she'd
shooed him outside to "keep an eye on things."

He'd watched from the deck, curious as to how Kat's
sons would react to the news of the coming week's arrangements. Both appeared to react favorably. The
younger one actually jumped up and down with joy and
wrapped his arms around Char's thighs in a quick hug.

The elder, Tag, glanced Jack's way—his look pen-
sive. Jack figured he was trying to work out all the
angles. Jack had been a little older when his father's
troubles started, but he'd found that kids sensed what
was happening no matter how diligently their parents
tried to keep the truth from them.

But whatever Jenna was saying seemed to work like
a balm on the boy's suspicions, because within minutes
Tag was grinning with obvious excitement. He looked
more like his mother when he smiled. Except for his
teeth. Even from a distance, Jack could tell the kid was
a candidate for braces.

As he watched the fivesome turn and head back to the house, Jack felt very much the outsider. He knew why. He not only lacked the desire to connect with Kat's children, he didn't have the slightest idea how to go about it if he were so inclined. He'd painted himself into a proverbial corner and he didn't possess a key to the door behind him. Not that he'd use it if he had one, but…

"Are you sure your sons are okay with this?" he asked Kat as she returned from the adjoining laundry room. She stopped abruptly, as if surprised to see him.

And why wouldn't she be? All he seemed capable of was following her around like a puppy dog.

She picked up a small yellow sponge and rubbed at an invisible spot on the countertop. "They're kids. And male. Both get to do something unexpected and fun— without their mother. What's not to like?"

"Well, they can't be too happy about me being here."

"Tag's the only one who caught that part of the deal."

She squeezed the water from the sponge with more force than seemed necessary, then turned to look at him. "He did ask if I was going to marry you."

Jack nearly swallowed his tongue. "Why?"

She shrugged. "I don't date. He's seen you here twice. I guess that qualifies as a serious relationship in his book." Her tone was light, but he sensed something broken and sad behind the sardonic chuckle. "Wanna finish off the cotton candy on the deck?"

Not really. He'd already eaten a chocolate sundae he didn't want. "Okay."

She opened a cupboard, rising on the toes of her cheap rubber thongs to reach a fluorescent-blue bag. "Grab a couple of waters from the fridge," she ordered.

He did as asked. When he turned to face her, a bottle in each hand, she told him, "We wash and reuse bottles. That's tap water. Hope you don't mind."

"I recycle under threat of never hearing the end of my boorish waste from my sister. I say, 'Bring it on.'"

Her laugh seemed genuine. "I'm really lucky to be living in a time when being cheap can pass as environmentally conscious."

Her admission was so Kat. Honest and unpretentious. Slightly apologetic when, in fact, the world should have been apologizing to her. He realized with sudden clarity that he would have fallen head over heels in love with her at that moment. If he weren't in love with someone else. Katherine. The schoolteacher. The woman of his dreams.

Ever since that night in Custer, he'd found himself thinking about Katherine—a victim of fate, yet so brave and resilient—at all the wrong times. On his bike in traffic. Placing a bet at the blackjack table. While taking a walking tour of Lead.

Had Katherine visited the nearby mining town when she lived in Deadwood? he asked himself. Right before he remembered that she wasn't real and he was losing his mind.

Kat was real. She wasn't Katherine, but she certainly was desirable. Sexy.

Kat regretted inviting Jack outside the moment he joined her at the railing of the small deck. She wished she didn't feel like jumping out of her skin every time he accidentally touched her. But she did.

"Wanna grab a chair?" she asked, pulling one of the four molded-plastic deck chairs from the stack in the corner. She dropped it in her usual spot and sat, kicking off her flip-flops to rest her heels on the top railing. The white-painted wood looked about as chipped and peeling as Jack's tattoo.

The sight had made her faintly queasy when he'd shown it to her earlier. Now more than ever she was glad she'd thrown the black ink in with the hazardous waste. Jack's were the last black tattoos she planned to give.

He sat beside her. A little too close, but she refrained from saying so.

"Are your tats still itchy?" she asked, wiggling her toes in the slight breeze. The night was warm but not muggy.

"Not bad. The antihistamine helped. No lasting ill effects."

We hope.

Kat didn't want to talk about her decision, but he deserved to know. Just in case.

"You asked me a question earlier and I sort of avoided answering."

"I noticed," he said, his tone amused. A refreshing change that she didn't expect to last.

She let her feet drop to the deck, then she turned to face him. "Listen. I don't expect you to understand something I don't entirely get myself, but…um…I was all set to go into the clinic. I told myself it was the smart thing to do, given the circumstances, but then…I didn't go."

"May I ask why?"

He sounded serious. Maybe even concerned, but at least he wasn't shouting or looking for something to punch the way her father did when he was upset. He'd never struck her, but she'd lost track of the times a beer bottle went flying across the room when he and her mother were arguing.

She looked at Jack a minute longer. His brow was gathered in a questioning look, but he didn't appear coiled and ready to explode. Kat actually felt safe enough to try to explain her rationale. "My mother has always said things happen for a reason. I used to think that was Mom's excuse for all the wrong turns she made in life. I promised myself I was going to plan better and not let my life be subject to the whims of fate. But—" she took a deep breath and let it out "—apparently I *am* my mother's daughter."

His head tilted slightly as if trying to figure out her meaning.

"I slept with you that night, Jack. I didn't plan to. If I had, I would have brought along birth control. I'm a savvy woman of today. I know about STDs. I'm not embarrassed to walk into a store and buy condoms. But sex was so far from my mind—" She stopped when she noticed his frown. She'd hurt his feelings.

Reaching out, she touched his arm. The way she might comfort Jordie. "I don't mean that you're not a sexy, desirable guy, Jack. You are." Her fingers were tingling in a very un-motherlike way. Swoo alert. She pulled back her hand. "But that night you were puffy and itchy and practically comatose. I still can't believe you managed to… Never mind."

He snickered softly, adding to her surprise. What was with this guy? Didn't he ever get mad?

"Maybe I wasn't myself," he said cryptically. "But given that we made love without benefit of birth control, certain repercussions might follow. And you led me to believe that you were going to eliminate that possibility."

"I know," she said, looking down. "I planned to. But there was a voice in my head that said you wound up in my bed for a reason. I don't know why, but I didn't feel right about trying to undo that, regardless of what happens."

Neither spoke for several minutes, then Jack asked, "So…if you wound up pregnant, did you plan on calling me?" His tone was faintly accusatory.

At last. A reaction she could understand. "Of course," she said defensively. "As complicated as it would probably be having a long-distance father in the picture, you and the baby still deserve to know each other."

He turned his chair to face her, then leaned forward, elbows on his knees. In that angle, she could only see his silhouette clearly. And his profile was so clearly Mad Jack's her heart started pounding like a long-distance runner's. The pulse in her head made it hard to make out what he was saying.

"…get one thing straight, Kat. I never planned to have children. Your sons will attest to the fact I'm not a daddy kind of guy. But if our being together that night created a baby, I *will* be a serious part of that child's life. I firmly believe in taking responsibility for one's actions—even if that means one of us has to move."

She swallowed harshly and tried to regain her composure. So many thoughts were racing through her brain she could barely pick which one to focus on. The word *move* lingered long enough for her to grab it.

"Move?" she cried, her voice a full octave higher than normal. "Are you serious? I can't move. Tag's dad would come unglued. Drew is a little more laid-back where

Jordie is concerned, but even *he* would take me to court if I tried to leave the area before his son turns eighteen."

His gunslinger—no, swimmer—shoulders lifted and fell. "Still, moving a family would be simpler than moving my entire business."

"Ha," she snorted. "You don't know my family. Not only do I have two sons and two spoiled ex-husbands, my mother's sick. Throat cancer. And my father's totally unpredictable. My older stepsiblings think he's crazy— too many years of hitting the bottle. I'm more inclined to blame it on cussed orneriness, but if I left, who would make sure he didn't sell off all the bison? Half the herd is mine. I can't leave them."

His mouth dropped open once or twice, but instead of a reply, he started to laugh. His reaction was so contrary to the fight she'd been expecting, all she could do was stare. For a moment. Then it struck her that he was laughing at her. People had been poking fun at her expense for years. Silly little Kat. Foolish girl most likely to screw up. Her bottom lip started to quiver and she had to blink fast to keep the tears back.

Jack's laughter stopped as quickly as it started. "What's wrong? Are you crying?"

Damn. Her neighbor's burglar-proof exterior spotlight was probably shining right on her face. "N-no. But it's not nice to laugh at—"

He cut her off by reaching out and taking her hand. "I'm sorry, Kat. I didn't mean to hurt your feelings, but you have to admit, worrying about the bison is a pretty unusual excuse for not leaving an area. Why do you think your father would get rid of them?"

She sniffled and pulled her hand free to brush away

the stupid tear that had formed in the corner of her eye. "I got sucked into the story of the bison when I studied history in high school. I spent months finding out everything I could about the animals, and then I located a small herd that was for sale. I begged Dad to buy them. To my profound surprise he did. But he's never let me forget that *my* animals are eating *his* grass and feed—even though Tag and Jordie and I are the primary ones who check on the herd and make sure they're okay."

She smiled, picturing the herd that had more than tripled in size over the years. "They're amazing animals. Healthy. Well adapted to the land. Just give them water and room to graze and they take care of the rest."

Jack was watching her with the same look she'd seen on her father's face when she started talking bison. "I'm hoping that when Tag and Jordie are old enough, we'll be able to sell part of our share and buy some land. Dad isn't going to live forever and you never know from one day to next whether you're in his will or on his buffalo chip list."

"Buffalo chip list," he repeated, his tone still decidedly amused. "Okay, I concede. Relocating a herd of bison might be more difficult than moving half-a-dozen dentists. But just barely."

She edged out of the direct light and stood to lean her lower back against the railing. What did a person say to that kind of agreeableness? Why wasn't he arguing? Where was the bluster and name-calling that always came in a fight?

He took a leisurely drink from his reused plastic bottle. She just didn't get him. Which was a surprise in and of itself. Mostly the men in her life followed a recognizable pattern of behavior. They wanted something from her, took it, then left. Period.

Jack was different.

He joined her at the railing, their shoulders a respectable distance apart. "I have a favor to ask, Kat."

Finally. Here it comes. Can you help me out with a load of laundry in the morning, honey? Could you spot me a few bucks till I get home? Do we really have to sleep in separate rooms, sweetie pie? It's not like we haven't already done the evil deed.

"I know you're busy, but do you think you could show me the bison before I leave?"

"Huh? You don't believe there's a herd."

"No. Of course, I believe you. I just want to see one. A real live North American bison. On the hoof, not packaged in my grocery store."

"Why?"

"Because they're bison, and..." His tone was so wistful he reminded her of Jordie, who shared Kat's passion for the animals. She understood completely, but she held her breath as she waited for him to finish.

"...I don't know. Latent guilt, I think."

"Pardon?"

He took another drink from his water bottle. His throat moved in a masculine, sexy way that had been her undoing more than once in the past. "I told you how much I love history, but one of the things I've never really been able to get my mind around is the massacre of the buffalo. I've forgotten the exact numbers, but there were millions of head roaming these lands before the white hunters came." His head shook slowly from side to side. "I feel like I need to apologize, but I've never seen a bison."

She took a drink, too. The cold liquid helped take her mind off her sudden, all-too-urgent desire to reach out and kiss him. He was a nice guy, but he wasn't the *right* guy. He might give lip service about honoring the big woolly beasts she'd come to love, but a few minutes with her dad would change that. Hell, two hours with her father had been all it took to put a rifle in peace-loving Drew's hand. Before the day was out, her new husband had his first kill. An innocent jackrabbit with nothing on its mind but dinner and a little procreation.

She knew what would happen if she took Jack to her father's ranch. She had nothing to lose, so she told him, "Sure. One day this week. I'll let you know." She turned to leave. "I gave you the extra key, right? I like to lock up at night. The neighbor's dogs would probably tell me if someone drove up, but why take chances?"

And she was all about playing it safe. Which was exactly why she was going to bed. Alone.

CHAPTER TWELVE

KAT HAD VACILLATED about taking Jack to see the bison for four days. Not because of the forty-five-minute drive and her current state of exhaustion—she was used to running on very little sleep—but because it might mean bumping into her father. She hadn't seen Buck in a month, although she usually called him once a week. Kat used the herd as an excuse to check up on him.

Buck, whose real name was Buford Earl Garrity, rarely initiated a call. In the past the only time he phoned anyone was when he was drunk. She'd thought about giving him a heads-up before they left the house but decided against it. As far as she knew, he was still alive. And sober. And if they bumped into him today, so be it, but she wasn't going out of her way to introduce him to Jack. Why hasten the inevitable?

"Stay in the car. I'll get the gate," she said, opening her door. "We can't hang around long and I'm not sure where the herd is. I hope this wasn't a waste of time."

Time. Precious time. So much to do, and yet here she was, trying to please Jack because she felt she owed him for being so nice to her and helpful at Thunder Alley. His presence alone seemed enough to keep the really persistent drunks away. And more than a few of the lady bikers seemed attracted to him. They drifted past her booth to flirt with Jack and wound up getting a henna tattoo.

Her profits were mounting. Which was a good thing because not only had her usually like-clockwork period not arrived, she woke up this morning to discover her nipples felt overly sensitive. She told herself the latter was a result of the dream she'd had. Her and Mad Jack on the prairie. Making love. Nothing but bare skin and blue sky. The sensuality of the breeze on her skin had been enough to— "I'm sorry. What did you say?"

She had her hand on the gate but hadn't opened the complicated contraption when she realized Jack had gotten out of the car and was approaching.

"Over there. Is that the herd?"

She stood on tiptoe to see where he was pointing. A slight hillock between her and the pasture that interested him blocked her view. She put her booted foot on the bottom strand of barbed wire beside the weathered wood post and hoisted herself up. Squinting against the early-morning brightness, she followed his outstretched arm.

He stepped close. Their bodies were almost touching, and for a split second she remembered her dream. Jack's body was a lot like his dream counterpart, even if they were miles apart in every other way.

"I thought at first they were cows, but then I spotted that big one. Is that the alpha male?"

"That's them, but they're a few head short. I wonder where…" She stretched upward and the wire she was standing on pulled loose from the post. She slipped.

It was just a few inches, but the rusty barbed wire could have meant a bad scratch at the very least. Fortunately Jack caught her. His arm went around her middle in a graceful swoop and he stepped away to keep both of them from getting hurt.

Her back was tight against his front. Their hearts were nearly level, and even through their clothing she could feel his speed up from the adrenaline. Her heart was beating fast, too. Probably from a different cause. She didn't want to think about it because if she did, she'd have to admit that Jack was growing on her. She thought about him more than she thought about Mad Jack. And in this morning's dream, for the first time, the two seemed to blur. One second she was kissing her wild and dangerous gunslinger, the next her sweet, charming orthodontist.

She was very confused. But one thing Kat knew for sure was that she wasn't making the same mistake she'd made with her ex-husbands. No matter what.

She wriggled free of his hold. "Thanks. Dad needs to do some fence work."

Jack appeared ready to say something, but a loud *put-put-put* sound made them both turn to locate the source.

"Oh, nuts. Here comes my dad. I was hoping we could sneak in and out without running into him."

"Why?"

"You'll see," she muttered softly. Or maybe he wouldn't. Both her ex-husbands were still friends with Buck. They hunted his land every fall and usually wound up staying overnight after partying a little too hard. Buck could drink anybody under the table.

"Hey, Daughter. I thought that was your car. Who's that with you?"

Buck Garrity looked every bit the larger-than-life

western rancher he portrayed himself as. Six-four in his youth. Three hundred pounds at his heaviest. His first family—a complex mix in its own right—was practically raised and his wife dead when he met and married Kat's mother. Despite the toll alcohol had taken on his liver, an ongoing battle with gout and some concerns about his heart, he exuded a rugged, healthful vibrancy that her mother still called the most powerful swoo on the planet.

"Jack, this is my father, Buck Garrity. Jack is from Denver. He's renting Tag's room from me this week because he was too late to find a place for the rally. I told you this in the phone message I left a few days ago. Do you ever check your messages?"

Her dad didn't answer. Nor had she expected him to. He opened the gate and walked out to shake Jack's hand. To Kat's surprise, Jack didn't appear the least bit intimidated or cowed.

"Nice to meet you. I was curious about the bison and Kat was nice enough to show me your herd."

"*Her* herd," Buck corrected. "I gotta admit I never would have bought 'em if she hadn't pestered me to do it. Now I can't picture the place without them. They're funny beasts. Smart and curious in a way cows aren't. Did she tell you about 'em?" he asked, motioning for Jack to follow.

Kat stifled her groan. This was so like her father. If he was in the mood, he could be as charming as any politician. And no one had ever accused him of being dumb. He knew more about bison than Kat could ever hope to know. For that reason alone, she hung back.

Her father noticed. He stopped midsentence and

looked at her. "I almost forgot. Your aunt called here looking for you. Needs you to call her back."

Kat frowned. There'd been a message on her machine when she got home last night, but it had been after midnight when she listened to it. Something about her mother's breathing.

Aunt Roberta had moved in with her mom about a year ago after her husband passed away. The two sisters hadn't talked in years—some hurt feelings or family blow-up—but when mom was diagnosed with throat cancer and needed help, Roberta sold her home in Iowa and moved to Spearfish, where Kat's mother lived.

Roberta was a nice woman, but she lacked her older sister's energy or imagination. Kat was afraid her mother might die of boredom, but she didn't say so, since Kat herself wasn't in a position to nurse her mom back to health.

"Can I use your phone, Dad?"

Buck unclipped the cell phone he wore at his waist and handed it to her. Then he turned back to his guest. "Bison are like elephants," he started. "They're a matriarchal herd with an alpha female, and they have a pecking order like chickens."

Elephant chickens. That was what Tag used to call them when Jordie was little.

Smiling to herself, Kat glanced at the two men one more time before heading to the car to call her long-winded aunt. Her gaze met Jack's. There was something deep and unreadable in his look. Pure swoo. Her knees buckled, but fortunately she was close enough to the fender to reach out for support.

Her heart sped up and suddenly she felt too warm.

She quickly punched in her aunt's number. "Hi, Roberta. It's me. Sorry I didn't call last night. I'm working my booth at the Alley and got in real late. Is Mom okay? Can I talk to her?"

"Oh, good. It's you, Kat. I was afraid I'd miss you today. Your mother is resting at the moment. We had a little scare last night. She was having trouble breathing. I called 9-1-1."

"Really? It was that bad?"

Her aunt sighed. "Probably not, but your mother couldn't tell me not to. She could barely whisper."

Roberta wasn't a decision-maker. "I'm so sorry I wasn't there to help. What happened?"

"The EMTs gave her some oxygen. That helped a lot. They wanted to take her to the hospital, but you know your mother. Once she could talk, she said no. But I'm taking her to the doctor today. At the very least, we need to have one of those bottles of oxygen around."

Kat breathed a silent sigh of relief. Her mother had fought back from the horrible diagnosis and surgery for throat cancer. She'd made it through chemo and radiation. But her will to live had suffered greatly these past nine months.

In a way, Kat understood. Her mother believed she needed a man in her life. And now she felt unattractive, unworthy of love. Kat's heart broke for her, but she didn't know how to change Mom's core belief.

"Thanks for calling, Roberta. I'm really sorry I'm not there to help, but tell Mom I love her. I'm at the ranch at the moment and I could maybe swing by on my way back to town but—"

"We won't be here, honey Kat. We'll be at the

doctor's office. Just try to check in from time to time. You can call me late, if you need to. I know how busy you are. Your mom knows, too. Don't worry. Things happen the way they're supposed to."

That truism again, Kat thought, closing the phone after saying goodbye. Her entire family had turned into fatalists. They'd never been very religious, although they'd attended church sporadically, depending on her mother's needs at the time. One of Kat's stepfathers had been a minister. Her mother used to say she'd fallen in love with his message, then learned too late that he didn't believe it.

Holding the phone firmly, she jogged after the two much smaller figures that were approaching the sixty or so head of bison scattered about a small bowl-shaped valley. The matriarch watched them intently. Younger bulls snorted nervously. Babies scampered awkwardly to their feet and huddled close to their mothers.

The men had stopped moving, so Kat was able to catch up rather quickly. "How come they're so close to the ranch, Dad?"

"Don't know. We cut and tagged half the cattle last week so I could supply some stock for the Deadwood rodeo. Maybe they were wondering what was happening."

"You didn't take out any of the bison, did you?" She and her father had had this argument many times over the years. She was never positive he respected her wishes.

"Naw. The only one they wanted was Leon. And he's too much trouble to move."

He pointed to a massive bull nibbling on a tuft of grass. The beast's shaggy mane gave him that definable look most people associated with bison. No one knew his exact age, since they bought him from a petting zoo with dubious records, but he was a majestic-looking beast. Most of the other animals were younger.

Now that she had a better view of the herd she could tell the numbers looked right. It wasn't that she didn't trust her father to care for the animals—and some losses happened no matter what—but she'd always felt that because she was who she was, the herd ran some risk of being ignored to death. Or casually sold at market. Not because Buck needed the money or was tired of the work. Simply because he could. She'd seen her father do all sorts of petty acts to hurt her mother—and her by association. Kat didn't want her beloved bison to become a pawn in a power game.

"It's getting late, Jack."

"Don't tell me you're doing that silly brown stuff again. What a racket!" Buck exclaimed, shaking his head so hard his straw cowboy hat nearly fell off. "Anybody dumb enough to get a tattoo in the first place is smart enough to only pay for it once."

Instead of looking embarrassed as she'd expected, Jack laughed. "Not all of us." He pushed up his sleeve and showed the faint shadow of what had been barbed wire. "Your daughter is an artist and she does a real steady business."

"What the hell? She got you to try one of those henna things?" He spat for good measure.

Jack snickered. "I wish. She tried to talk me into the henna, but I had to do it my way. Brought my own ink. It must have been old and mixed with gasoline or something because I wound up sicker than a dog."

Her father obviously couldn't believe a real man

would do such a thing. His mouth still hung partly open. "Why didn't you just go to a legitimate tattoo parlor?"

Jack shrugged. "Needles. Can't stand needles."

"Oh," her father said, like a true kindred spirit. "Me, neither. But that brown stuff is just too girly for my taste."

Kat laughed for the first time in her father's presence in she didn't know how long. Even hearing him say the word *girly* sounded funny to her. For a man who claimed not to care what people thought of him to worry about being emasculated by a temporary tattoo struck her as ridiculous. But in a way, it made sense.

Suddenly something clicked in her head and she understood that no matter how she lived her life or what she accomplished, her father would still make judgment calls based on his own sense of what mattered.

Both men were staring at her, she realized. She didn't care. "See you later, Dad. Oh, and by the way, Mom's not doing too hot. Just FYI."

"You know I hate abbreviations," her dad said with a growl.

"TDB," she said with a small wave.

Jack hurried to catch up. "TDB?" he repeated softly. "I don't know that one."

"Too damn bad."

His laugh made the matriarch of the herd give a loud snort, and a second later the entire herd was on the move. Kat could hear her father muttering as she locked the gate behind them, but for once in her life, she honestly didn't care what her father thought. Period.

TDB, Jack thought, looking out the side window at the rolling landscape as Kat drove them back to her home. The green pastures dissected by cultivated farmland and small ranches reminded him of northeastern Colorado. He'd thought about moving to Fort Collins out of college, but his mother had convinced him Denver had more opportunities. He liked Denver, but he was sorry now that he hadn't at least tried somewhere new so he could say he had.

"Your father's a real character," he said.

"That's a polite way to put it. Although both my exes get along great with him. He's what you might call a man's man. Like John Wayne."

Jack nodded. "Yeah. I can see the comparison. I've never been a big John Wayne movie buff. Although my mom gave me a complete set of his Westerns for Christmas, and I have to admit, some of them aren't bad."

He turned to look at her. The way she was working that bottom lip told him she was deep in thought. Planning. Juggling. Trying to fill everyone's needs except her own. He'd never met anyone like her. Always ready to help, even when she was exhausted. And she had to be. He was pooped just from trying to keep up with her.

"We're stopping at the house before heading to Blood Alley, right?"

That made her smile. He'd seen enough fistfights, fender benders and drunks with blood running down their faces the past couple of days to make him rename Thunder Alley.

"Yes. So you can get your bike. I'm not opening the booth until later this afternoon. One of Char's friends is holding down the fort for me. He does Lakota painting."

"Where are you going, if you don't mind my asking?"

She hesitated long enough to make him think she might, but she answered, "Sentinel Pass. To see Libby.

You heard about Coop's big party on Sunday, right? The whole town is invited."

"Yeah. You mentioned it the other day, but I never heard what kind of party it is. Birthday?"

"No. A belated wedding party. He feels guilty about how fast he and Lib got married. Everyone in Sentinel Pass knows Lib and would have been invited if it wasn't for the paparazzi, so now he's going to do a big bash for all the locals."

"This coming Sunday?"

She nodded.

"Libby asked you to help?"

She nodded.

"And you told her, 'No. Sorry. I can't take on anything else because I'm already running myself ragged.'"

He could tell by the way her eyes widened behind her sunglasses that he hadn't done a good job of disguising his sense of outrage on her behalf. Even Kat's father seemed to think nothing of making demands on his daughter's time, despite the fact that she was juggling any number of jobs, raising two kids alone and going to school. And the guy was rich. While Kat had been on the phone, Buck had described in detail his recent safari adventure. Trips like that didn't come cheap.

Jack's father, for all his faults, had been one of the most generous men Jack had ever known. His mother might attach a few strings to her gifts, but not his dad. He just gave and gave. The fact that the boy who'd accused Dad of inappropriate behavior had been a pro bono case had seemed to irk Jack's mother more than anything. Why, he wasn't sure.

"By help," Kat said, drawing his attention back to the

present, "I plan to show up and do some creative mingling. Quite a few of the crew members will have arrived in town by then, and Libby's afraid the two factions will wind up sitting on opposite sides of the street and never interact."

"What about your booth?"

"I never work on Sundays unless the boys can be with me. We usually go to church, then do something that can't be misconstrued as work. Hiking the Michelson Trail or swimming at Sheridan Lake. Or renting a bunch of movies. I don't work *all* the time."

"Hmm. Sorry I got all defensive on your behalf."

She smiled. "No problem. It was kinda sweet. Sounds like something Mad— Never mind. What do you think of the rally so far?"

Mad. She'd been about to say a name. Madeleine? Madonna? She didn't know about his dream, so it couldn't have been Mad Jack.

He put the thought out of his head and answered her question as diplomatically as possible. He couldn't tell her the truth. That he liked watching her work. That he hated the men who leered at her and the women who acted better than her. That he was falling in love with her and wasn't sure what to do about it.

She'd made it abundantly clear that he was not her type—whatever that meant. Some women were their own worst enemies. Even smart women, like Kat. And his sister, Rachel. They made choices based on superficial reasons and later were shocked by the depth of their regret.

Fine, he told himself. Kat's decisions were none of his business. This was his time to find himself and expand the boundaries that nearly caused him to make a choice based on the wrong reasons.

He'd learned from that near miss. He was his own man now. He hadn't talked to his sister or mother in three days, although he had texted them both to let them know he was okay. In his travels around Blood Alley, he'd observed unpleasantly naked people doing the kinds of things his ex participated in. So far this trip, he'd imbibed more than was wise, eaten ridiculously unhealthy food and, let's not forget, made love to a stranger. Hell, at this rate, he'd be Mad Jack before he left the Hills.

CHAPTER THIRTEEN

I'M PREGNANT.

Impossible though it seemed—the odds were so in her favor for once. They'd only made love the one time.

I mean, come on, she thought, scowling at her reflection in the mirror. The chances seemed infinitesimal.

But she'd awoken that morning with the truth in her head. Still no period and her nipples definitely felt chafed. And the thought of the smell of coffee left a bad taste in her mouth. And she was horny as hell.

All signs she couldn't ignore. The last had been her ex-husbands' favorite pregnancy side effect. Raging hormones blocked her normal inhibition and turned her into a much less repressed version of herself.

She looked around the door of the bathroom to check her bedside clock. Too early to make a trip to the pharmacy for a home pregnancy test. Not that she needed a little blue stick to confirm what she already knew. But Jack probably would.

Today was Sunday. Cooper's big party was scheduled for this afternoon, and Jack planned to take off after putting in an appearance—at Libby's request. He'd made reservations at a motel in Edgemont, the state-line town where he'd stayed on the way here from Denver.

She couldn't wait to pick up her sons. She missed Tag and Jordie so much she got a little weepy thinking about them. She'd talked to each boy every day and felt the experience of being away had been good for them, but she was so ready to have them back. If her friends would let them go.

Jenna couldn't say enough about Tag's work ethic and rapport with the tourists who came to the Mystery Spot. "He seems so much older than eight. Well, almost nine, as he tells all his coworkers. I think he has a crush on Robyn." Robyn Craine was Jenna's manager at the Mystery Spot. She was due to return to college in a couple of weeks, and Jenna was already sweating the loss.

Char seemed equally pleased with how her time with Jordie had turned out. "He's an awesome kid, Kat. If I had a kid, I'd hope he'd be just as cool."

There had been a funny catch in her friend's usually unflappable voice when they'd talked last night, but Kat had been too exhausted to question it.

This year's rally had nearly done her in. She'd worked through the heat, the wind and the quick summer squalls, in addition to the great horde of humanity that passed just beyond the flaps of her tent.

She'd seen everything from a woman who crashed her bike in front of Kat's tent and nearly decked the paramedic who came to her aid to several naked people doing things they'd never have done in public if they were at home. The only thing that really surprised her, though, was Jack. He rarely left her immediate vicinity. He was like a self-appointed watchdog. And his presence had felt surprisingly comforting.

Thank God for Jack, she'd thought more than once.

Now, she didn't know what to think. They hadn't really talked about what might happen if the inconceivable happened—she conceived. Although it was tempting to postpone the inevitable, she knew it would be easier to talk this out face-to-face rather than over the phone.

From previous experience—both of her exes would have jumped at the plan she was going to offer Jack—and given Jack's admitted aversion to children, she wasn't expecting him to want to be too involved. So if he'd kick in a reasonable amount of child support, she'd let him off the hook parenting-wise.

She swallowed the bad taste in her mouth and leaned over the sink to give her teeth another go with the toothbrush. The mint flavor helped, but not much. She got a little queasy thinking about what was in store for all of them, but they'd adjust. They'd get by. Just like always.

In the meantime, she had Plan A. She quickly fluffed her hair with wet fingertips and faked a smile. What she planned to do was wrong on so many levels she'd lost count, but darn it, the worst that could happen already had, so why the heck not give in to temptation and tell him goodbye in a way he'd never forget?

She looked down at the skimpy tank top she'd pulled on, braless. Her nipples, which truly had a mind of their own even when she wasn't pregnant, made two distinct dots against the stretchy white fabric. Two pregnancies notwithstanding, her breasts weren't bad. Mad Jack had called them perfect.

She sighed and shook her head. She wasn't going to think about him. She was going to seduce Jack. Jackson Boyd Treadwell. He'd given her his wallet to hold while he participated in some group tug-of-war the other day.

She'd peeked inside on the excuse she might need to know his blood type. A slightly dated group photo of Jack, his mother—Kat could tell by the eyes—and his sister was the only personal item he carried.

Despite their spending the better part of the past five days together, she didn't really know him. He was a pleasant, generous, nicely mannered enigma. With a great body, gorgeous masculine lips and a butt that really did look sexy in chaps.

He might not be the steely eyed gunslinger of her dreams, but he turned her on, and that seemed as good a reason as any for what she was planning to do.

With a final glance in the mirror, she left the bathroom. Her heart was pounding more than she would have liked. Through the open windows in the living room, she could hear birds singing. The sky still held that pinkish glow she loved best.

The cool breeze tickled her bare legs as she dashed down the hall. With the most minimum of knocks, she opened the door and leaned in far enough to make out Jack's outline on the bed. He slept on his side. Just like Tag. Pillow bunched under his head. Arm stretched out. The covers were pushed down to his waist. His chest was bare.

Her mouth went dry and her courage almost left her. But that indefinable something that got her into this mess in the first place felt more powerful than ever. Swoo. Desire. Hormones. She didn't know its name. And at the moment she didn't care. She just knew this would be her last chance to create a memory, not a dream.

Jack heard the door open, but he kept his eyes closed. Kat's house was so small and poorly built he'd actually heard her get out of bed and pace around a bit before brushing her teeth. He hadn't expected her to stop at his door, but she had. Now she was advancing slowly toward the bed.

He assumed that since he was leaving in a few hours, it was time for the I'm-not-pregnant-and-there's-really-no-reason-for-us-to-see-each-other-again talk. She'd adroitly managed to avoid the subject of their night together any time he tried to bring it up. He might have pressed harder if he hadn't observed that most people in Kat's life demanded things of her without any regard for her own agenda.

There was another reason he hadn't pushed her for an answer. He liked her. More than liked. He was ridiculously attracted to her. There was a distinct chance he was falling in love with her. Kat. Not Katherine, the woman in his dream. It had taken this week for him to see that Kat was everything Katherine was— and more. While both women were smart, witty and brave, Katherine projected a sort of self-contained perfection. Kat was far from perfect, but she put herself on the line in ways Mad Jack's schoolmarm would never dare.

Kat would take on any bully—even her father—to protect a friend...or her beloved bison. Unfaltering in her loyalty. Maddeningly single-minded when it came to her friends and family. The kind of person he wished his mother had been when his father had been in trouble.

Maybe somewhere along the way, he'd concluded that familial integrity only existed in yesteryear. His subconscious even provided the woman of his dreams. But then he met Kat. And reality was so much better.

Unfortunately she'd kept him at arm's length in a neat little box of her own design. He would have been hurt if he didn't understand exactly what she was doing—and why. He'd done the same thing with relationships all his life.

A board under her heel made a creaking sound and he used the cue to move. Trying not to overplay his role, he let out a muffled moan and rolled to his back.

"You're awake, aren't you?"

He kept his eyes closed, but he couldn't prevent a grin. "Maybe, but if you're naked, I'm pretty sure I'm dreaming."

She hopped onto the bed beside him. Her weight made the mattress sag just a little and he rolled toward her. "I'm not naked...but I could be...if you wanted me to be."

His eyes flew open. "Really?"

She wasn't nude, but the few scraps of cloth she was wearing were more provocative than she could possibly know. White tank top that dipped low across the tops of her breasts. Their fullness outlined in shadow, her nipples clearly erect. The shirt's hemline barely skimmed the elastic waistband of her French-cut panties. He could see a few golden-blond curls peaking out beneath the lavender silk.

He swallowed hard and shifted slightly so he didn't embarrass himself. "Tell me you're not here to—"

She leaned down and kissed him. "I'm here because I want to be. No hidden agenda. No strings. We're unattached people who like each other, I think. I'm not wrong, am I?"

Like truly didn't cover the depth of his feelings, but it was enough for now. He reached out and gently ran his hand along her cheek and jaw. "You're not wrong." Then he pulled back the sheet to welcome her closer.

The room was light enough for her to see his body's reaction to her offer. She didn't lie down beside him as he expected. Instead, she curled her feet under her and lifted up slightly to pull her tank top over her head. The sight of her beautiful bare breasts and lean, tanned torso made every ounce of testosterone in him surge through his blood.

"You are incredibly sexy," he said. "Gorgeous. Absolutely gorgeous."

Her cheeks were too pink. That didn't surprise him. He knew she didn't handle compliments well, but he couldn't help lavishing praise as he touched her. "Your skin is the prettiest color I've ever seen. Last time, I thought it was candlelight that gave it this warm, sunny glow, but no. This is you. Beautiful Kat."

She cocked her head in question. *Last time.* He didn't want to mention his fantasy woman, Katherine. Now was not the time to bring up another woman's name— even if she was a figment of his imagination and probably some subconscious incarnation of Kat.

To distract her, he took her hand and brought it to his lips. He kissed each fingertip, stained with henna. There wasn't a part of his body he wouldn't trust to her capable hands. He wanted to tell her that, but he didn't think she'd believe him.

She wriggled close enough for him to smell her warmth and raw sexual perfume. Need hit him at a gut level. It took all his self-control not to pin her below him and take what she appeared to be offering.

"I woke up horny," she said. "Foreplay is nice and all, but I'm...um...ready for whatever."

Not what he was expecting to hear. Not his shy, strait-laced Kat. He'd never even heard her swear. But when he looked in her shining blue eyes, he understood. This was about mutual need. The sexual tension that had been building all week wasn't one-sided.

"Then by all means, my dear, hop aboard," he said, flopping backward—exposed. Vulnerable.

She looked her fill and actually licked her lips. "Nice package," she said, her blush intensifying. "I understand that's the correct lingo these days. I don't remember looking that closely last time."

"Thanks. I aim to please."

"I can see that, but if you don't mind…I…um… Oh, heck, I'm just going to say this. You mentioned something about fantasies when I first met you. And that got me thinking about something I've wanted to try but didn't exactly know how—or who—to ask. Would you be up—no pun intended—for a little…um…bondage? Nothing kinky, just…"

The word threw him for a second. It reminded him of Jaydene. But only for a second. This was Kat. Sweet, shy, adorable Kat, who was offering him yet another chance to prove something to himself. If he dared.

He held out his hands, wrists together. "Anything you want. I'm your man."

Her grin lit up the room for a second before she vaulted from the bed. "I'll be right back."

She returned with two men's ties. One a sober blue. The other a gaudy paisley print. "I promise this won't hurt," she said, taking his left hand and stretching it out toward the knobby bedpost.

"I probably shouldn't admit this," she went on, "but

when I bought this bed for Tag, I actually thought the headboard had all sorts of possibilities." Her blush was so adorable he almost blurted out his love for her.

Not yet. Too soon. She wouldn't believe me.

"I promise not to tell him," Jack said. Like that kind of conversation would ever come up. He'd never talked sex with his dad, and couldn't imagine discussing the subject with someone else's kid.

She climbed over him to secure the other wrist. He watched as she made a quick, efficient flip of the wrist and pulled a loop through the knot. "Where'd you learn to tie so well?"

"The ranch. My dad didn't think I was smart enough to go to college, so he wanted me to have some marketable skills."

"Like tying up men?"

She laughed. "Like tying up horses."

She sat back and looked him over. "Cool. Now I pretty much have you at my mercy, don't I?"

He flexed first one arm, then the other. He definitely wasn't going anywhere. "I believe you do, Miss Katherine."

He winced. The name had slipped. He saw her eyebrows knit for a moment, then she shrugged lightly and straddled his waist. She wiggled provocatively. He wanted to touch those perfect breasts. But when he reached out, his arm stopped well short of her.

"Whoa. I don't think I like this. I can't touch you."

"Sure you can. But only the parts I let you touch." To prove her point, she leaned over and put his left hand on her breast. His right fingers came in contact with her leg.

He closed his eyes and stretched to get the most for

his reach. Then she moved again. She put her hands on either side of his face and leaned down to kiss him.

"I didn't expect this, you know," she told him, running her tongue across his bottom lip.

"Expect what?"

"Everything. You surprised me. On so many levels." She trailed tiny kisses down his neck and across the top of his collarbone. Her fingers played with his flat nipples until they stood rigid. Every sensation wreaked havoc on his self-control, but the ties around his wrists kept him from trying to take over the seduction.

This was happening on Kat's terms.

She tickled him lightly under the arms. He bucked as if she'd pinched him. "No fair. I'm ticklish. I admit it. Oh, crap, you're not going to use that against me, are you?"

She didn't answer. Instead, she slid downward until she was kneeling between his legs. She very gently dragged her fingernails across the sole of his foot. He practically levitated off the bed.

"This is so illuminating. Big, strong, motorcycle bad boy who picks fights in bars is ticklish. I could so use this against you if you were going…"

She didn't finish the thought. Instead, she looked in his eyes for a heartbeat or two, then slowly came forward, her gaze dropping to his waist. As she neared his middle, she licked her lips in a slow, provocative way that made his heart start to race. She lowered her mouth to his body, teasing the tip of his penis with her tongue before closing her lips around him.

Handicapped as he was, he had to acknowledge that he was at her mercy, but what sweet mercy it was. She used her teeth, her tongue, and…oh, yes, her mouth. "Kat!" he cried. "You're killing me."

He twisted and pulled against his constraints, which he realized did add an element of adventure he'd never imagined. He was all hers, in every way possible.

Panting with the strain of not coming, he begged her to let him go. "I need…hands…please…you…Kat. Kat." She pushed him to the edge of his restraint, then suddenly she pulled back and looked at him, a smoldering half-hooded look of satisfaction and lust on her face. She moved toward him again and a second later settled her body over his.

They'd done this before, and yet they hadn't. That first time had been in the dark, in a dream. This was real, undeniably real.

She put her hands flat against his chest and started to move in a primal circle of life, her hips lifting and falling, her vaginal walls tightening and releasing. Since he couldn't do anything else, he closed his eyes and lived each second, each sensation.

He'd never felt a buildup like this before. His release seemed to start in the far corners of his extremities and implode to his very core, making him buck his hips into her as fast and hard as he could. He had no idea if she was on the same plain as him. He wanted to please her and feel her mutual pleasure, but his orgasm was too mind-blowing. All he could do was shout her name as he gave in to the all-consuming sensations that he knew he'd never forget.

Kat collapsed against Jack's heaving chest. *Holy garbanzo beans!* she silently cried. Who knew that a couple of ties could add a whole other dimension to sex?

She had no idea where the nerve to suggest bondage came from—maybe his earlier hints that his ex-girlfriend had called their sex life boring. *Maybe I'm a closet control freak,* she thought, tucking her chin to keep him from seeing her smile.

Whatever the reason, the result was the best sex she could ever remember having. Talk about going out with a bang, she thought with satisfaction.

But there was no denying a bittersweet quality, too. The best sex ever was never going to happen again because Jack was leaving. The thought made her breath catch.

She lifted her head and looked at him. His eyes were open as if he was watching her, maybe trying to read her mind. She smiled. This had been her idea, her tiptoe over to the wild side. "You okay?"

He didn't answer, but when he gave the ties a little tug, she knew it was time to undo her handiwork. The knots were the quick-release kind and all she had to do was pull the free end and the fabric slithered to the sheets.

He blinked in surprise. "Wow. You're amazing. In ways I never imagined."

"Never?" She couldn't help feeling a little hurt. After all, they had had sex once before and it had been pretty good, too. She thought. Not quite as phenomenal as this time, but—

He pulled her to him and rolled to his side. "What I meant by that is I've never met anyone who could tie that particular kind of knot."

"Oh."

"And as for the way you made love to me…well, there simply aren't enough words. Unbelievable. In a good way. A great way. Am I making you mad?"

He must have felt her start to tense up. "No. Not really. I just think people have been underestimating me all my life. And I let them. You're less likely to be a disappointment that way."

The furrows in his brow told her he was pondering her statement but before he could say anything, a loud *beep-beep-beep* made them both startle. Tag's clock radio was set for Sunday-morning church.

She scrambled off the bed and hit the off button. The fact that she'd tied Jack up and had her way with him on her son's bed without even thinking about going to church on the morning she realized she was pregnant and unwed... She swallowed a small cry and looked around for her clothes.

"Are you running away again?"

A reference to her horrified reaction the last time they made love, no doubt. "We have a busy day ahead." She yanked on her panties and top. "I'll make coffee."

He caught her hand. "Kat, can you at least wait long enough for me to tell you I think you're amazing and that was the best sex I've ever had?"

Her, too, but she didn't turn around. "You promised to help me refold the tent and put it away."

He made a sound of pure exasperation and sat up. "Oh, no," he said, smacking his forehead with the heel of his hand. "We forgot birth control again."

Now. This was it. *If you can tie up a guy and have your way with him, you can tell him about the illegitimate baby you're going to have.* "I didn't forget. I just didn't bother. After all, you can only get pregnant once."

He frowned. "What's that me— Holy sh— You're not serious. You can be sure this soon?"

"I haven't taken the test, but I know my body."

She left him then. To think. To get his excuses in order.

She showered, got dressed and made coffee. A whole damn pot, which she realized too late she shouldn't drink and had to heat up water for caffeine-free tea. She was on her second cup when Jack entered the kitchen, familiar tote bag in hand.

He poured himself a cup. Black. Took a couple of quick sips, then set his mug on the counter and walked to the table where she was sitting. He pulled her chair out as if she wasn't on it and turned it so he could go down on one knee in front of her. "Kat, I know we don't know each other well, but—"

"If carnal knowledge counts, I know you better than I ever knew my second husband."

He gave her a serious look.

"Sorry."

"We know each other pretty well in several ways, but I'm asking you to marry me."

There hadn't been any mention of a shotgun. She gave him credit for that. But neither was there mention of love.

"Thank you, Jack. You're the closest thing to a hero I've ever known, but my answer is no, thank you."

He looked shocked. "Why not? I can provide for you...and the boys. I know there are logistics to work out, but—"

"I know all those things, Jack. And this week you've proved to me what a great guy you are. I hope we'll become good friends as our child grows up. But I can't marry you."

"Can't or won't?"

"Both."

"Why?"

"Because I'm holding out for the fantasy," she admitted, then wished she hadn't said the word out loud. A woman like her couldn't afford fantasies. "I know. That sounds silly and juvenile and I should probably put our unborn child's welfare first, but frankly, I tried that. Twice. And it didn't work. I wound up in the middle of a legal battlefield, the same way I was raised. I won't do that again. The next time I get married it's going to be for love."

He put out his hands. "But I love you."

She looked at the ceiling. "No, you don't. You're telling me that out of a sense of duty. You're a dutiful son, a responsible doctor and a good person, Jack. But I need to know that the man doing the asking wants me for the right reasons, not because he feels an obligation to a baby we accidentally made one night."

"Kat, I didn't expect any of this when I came here and I'm probably making a complete mess of my proposal, but I really have developed strong feelings for you. I think it's love."

He sounded so earnest she had to smile. "I appreciate that, Jack. Let me know when you're sure."

"You're being facetious."

She shrugged. "I've had good reason to be where the men in my life are concerned. I know you're not Pete Linden or Drew Petroski, but some of the mistakes I made in the past were because I didn't understand who I was and what I wanted out of life.

"I do now. I know that being a good mother to my children and becoming a teacher are important parts of who I am. I'm also a woman who deserves to be loved for who she is—mistakes and all. And until I find the right man, I'm not saying 'I do' again. Baby or no baby."

CHAPTER FOURTEEN

JACK PICKED a can of soda from a huge plastic barrel
filled with ice and soft drinks. There was a full bar with
a margarita machine set up on the grass behind the
Sentinel Pass fire station, but since he was headed back
on the road today, he decided to stay sober. Not to mention that his mind was still reeling from the morning.
Amazing sex *and* being told he was going to be a father?
Yeah, not your normal morning, he thought, looking for
Kat.

They'd driven separately to the party. She was meeting her kids here and she'd been positively giddy at the
prospect.

He spotted her near the silly concrete dinosaur. She
was holding Jordie, the littlest boy, on her hip while listening with rapt attention as the older boy told her something. She really was a wonderful mother. He didn't
have to worry about her caring for their child with equal
love and devotion. But was that enough?

He popped the tab on his drink and tasted the sweet,
cool liquid. His hand shook slightly and he felt the
strangest urge to cry. His dad had been gone so long, but
Jack could almost feel his presence. If he were here today, Jack knew what he'd say to him.

"I'm sorry, Dad. You were the best pop a kid could ask for, and I'm sorry I even once doubted that you were innocent. I wanted to believe you. I told myself I believed, but then a tiny bit of doubt would creep in and I'd ask myself, 'Why didn't he have an assistant working with him that day? Why'd he go to the office alone? Was he trying to hide something?'"

Jack lifted the can to his lips and forced himself to swallow past the lump in his throat. His guilt had been there at the back of his mind for years. His father passed away without either of them talking about Jack's doubts. Now, of course, it was too late.

But Jack never once questioned that he and his sister, Rachel, had been the most important people in their father's life. Yes, Dad had adored—*worshiped* might even have been the right word—their mother, but that relationship was complex and beyond young Jack's ken. His father's steadfast love, though, had carried Jack through some really rough times. If he and Kat were going to have a child, then Jack owed it to his father— and himself—to be the best father he could be. As scary and life-changing as that sounded.

"Hey," a voice said. "You're Kat's friend, aren't you?"

Jack turned to look at the man addressing him. It took him a second to place the guy. He'd been behind the wheel of the truck the day Jack and Kat visited Sentinel Pass. "Yeah. Jack Treadwell. You're Libby's brother, right? The miner."

The guy gave a snorting sound that probably qualified as a laugh. "Mac McGannon." They shook hands. Mac's were rough and huge. They never would have fit inside a patient's mouth. "Mining has turned into a hobby now that I have a rich brother-in-law. Coop thinks we'll make more money off it by building a B and B on the property and giving mine tours."

"That sounds like easier work."

"Not if you're not crazy about people," he said wryly. "Just look at all these strangers. And the real tourists won't start coming until after the television show airs." He shook his head with a certain degree of resignation. "Times are changing. 'Course, it's been that way for a while. The old ones die and their families sell out, instead of coming back here to live. Maybe this boost to the economy will bring new families in." He frowned. "Doesn't look good to have houses sitting empty. Fire risk, for one thing."

Jack noticed for the first time the volunteer fire-department logo on the man's black T-shirt. They talked a bit longer about what kinds of challenges small communities like Sentinel Pass were experiencing. "We had a doctor here years ago when I was a kid," Mac said, his dark eyes checking from time to time on the where-abouts of a little girl who seldom left her aunt's side.

Kat had told him the tragic tale of Mac's wife, who, on the verge of leaving him for another man, crashed her car into a ravine and died. Fortunately Mac had refused to let his wife take their daughter with her when she left. A four-year-old beauty. Jack couldn't remember her name.

"Just out of curiosity, are there a lot of houses for sale around here?" Jack asked.

An idea had started to take shape in his mind as Mac spoke of the community and its possible rebirth. Sentinel Pass wasn't Denver, but Jack had been ready for a change at so many levels for so long it wasn't surprising that he was starting to look at the place with new eyes.

Mac thought a moment. "Mrs. Smith's place is going on the market tomorrow, I heard. She passed away a couple of months ago. Her son and daughter have been trying to decide what to do with the place. They've been renting it to Shane and Coop." He pointed to a very recognizable blond guy across the plaza and a dark-haired fellow Jack had never seen before. "Shane's the writer, producer, director…hell, I don't know what he does. He and Jenna are together."

Jack could see that. Not only were they holding hands and talking with an intimacy that belonged to people in love, they had a dog. An enormous, gorgeous beast with black, white and rust-colored markings. The animal seemed perfectly trained, because it watched the children filing in and out of the bounce house that had been erected in the parking lot, but never made any effort to chase them.

"Anyway, I was just talking to Jill and Peter. They had a real-estate agent from Rapid give them a market appraisal. Makes sense to sell, since neither of their families wants to live here."

Jack nodded. A flutter of excitement coursed through his body. He didn't make crazy, impulsive leaps of faith. But he knew someone who did. Mad Jack. And he didn't even have to ask what Mad Jack would do. He knew the answer. "Are they still here? Mrs. Smith's kids?"

Mac looked around. "Right over there, talking to Elana Grace. She owns the Tidbiscuit. Our local answer to Starbucks," he added dryly. He squinted slightly as he looked a moment longer. "I don't know who the gal in the hat is. She didn't come with Jill and Peter. Maybe she's one of the TV people, although she looks kind of familiar…"

Jack checked her out. Beauty-queen posture. Same Ann Taylor-kind of skirt and blouse his ex-fiancée might have worn. The straw sunhat looked chic and expensive. Jaydene definitely would have been able to identify the brand of purse she was carrying.

"No one I know, which I guess isn't surprising since this is only my second time in town," he said.

He wiped his hand on his pants and held it out. Mac didn't notice at first, his attention still trained on the stranger. "Oh. Sorry," he said, quickly shaking Jack's hand.

"No problem. I appreciate the tip about the house. I've been thinking about relocating to the Hills. This might work out."

Mac's coal-black eyebrows rose in unison. He glanced in the general direction of where Kat had been standing, then returned his gaze to Jack. Jack half expected him to ask something he wasn't prepared to talk about, but instead, Mac said, "Libby called you a stand-up guy. That's good enough for me."

Mac started to leave, but Jack stopped him. "Um...I know I'm getting ahead of myself, but do you know who I'd call about putting in a pool?"

Mac looked only slightly abashed, but he recovered quickly. "Me. I got a backhoe just sitting at the mine collecting dust now that my brother-in-law is my partner. Number's in the book. Give me a call when you're ready."

His low chuckle stayed with Jack, but it wasn't the sound that had tormented him as a kid. It was okay. Inclusive, even. He had a feeling he and Mac McGannon might be friends one day.

But first, he had a house to buy.

Kᴀᴛ ᴡᴀᴛᴄʜᴇᴅ Jack conversing with Mac as covertly as she could manage, but apparently she wasn't subtle enough to avoid Char's acute observation skills. "You've been nailed by some serious dentist swoo, haven't you?"

Before Kat could deny the charge, Tag, who had been counting some of the tips he'd earned from working for Jenna, looked at them and said, "That guy's a dentist?"

"Orthodontist," Kat corrected. "He straightens teeth."

Tag gave her a look. "I know what an orthodontist is. You and Dad have been fighting about sending me to one long enough."

Kat felt a blush coming on. She hadn't realized Tag was aware of her ongoing argument with Pete, who believed that their son's crooked baby teeth weren't worth the hassle and expense of getting straightened. She'd agreed to wait until his permanent teeth started coming in, but now it was obvious Tag had inherited her family's crooked teeth. Kat didn't know how she'd managed to avoid braces, but she thanked her lucky stars since neither of her parents probably would have noticed— even if her teeth looked like Tag's.

"We both agree you'll need braces, Tag. We just can't agree on the timing," she told him.

"Or who will pay," Char added.

Kat gave her a dirty look. She'd overheard way too many shouting matches about who owed what when she was a kid. Tag deserved better. And once she was a teacher with a decent salary and possibly even dental benefits, she'd take him in—even if his father claimed he couldn't afford to pay half.

"Did I hear someone say *braces?*" a familiar voice asked. "Hi, Char. Tag."

Tag nodded, but didn't greet Jack until he spotted Kat's severe stare. Manners counted. Period. Tag knew that. "Hey. Where's your bike?"

"Next to the fire station. Mac said it was okay to leave it there. I…uh…have a couple of Rally T-shirts in the side pouch for you and your brother. If you want 'em. No big deal. Just thought…"

Kat was surprised. And touched. She hadn't seen him buy the gifts and hadn't expected him to, but she could tell by Tag's smile he was intrigued. Maybe even willing to forget that he didn't like this R.U.B. who'd been renting his room.

"Cool. When I can I see it?"

Kat looked at Jack, who appeared to be studying Tag with an intent frown on his face. His gaze never left her son's mouth.

Uh-oh. Orthodontist alert.

"Right now," Jack said, his tone casual. But Kat was attuned enough to him to know he was thinking about something else. "It's the only bike there. The saddlebag is snapped shut. Help yourself… Uh, sorry. If that's okay with your mother, I mean."

Kat looked at Char trying to convey a leave-us-for-a-second message. "This is Sentinel Pass. Nobody's gonna steal him or any… Oh, okay. Come on, Taggart. Let's go find your brother. He'll want his present, too."

"Thanks. And, Tag, come right back to thank Jack. Jordie, too."

"I know, Mom."

Kat watched her eldest son walk away. He was getting so grown up. A week with Jenna had changed him. He seemed more confident and aware of the world around him. He wasn't her little boy anymore.

"He needs to see an orthodontist," Jack said without preamble. "Bring him to Denver and I'll do X rays and an initial evaluation for free."

For free. He knew her well.

Instead of being offended, as some people might have been, she was thrilled by the offer. But she had to turn him down. Again. Just as she had his proposal.

"I'm all set to play an extra in the filming this week. It's good money. With the you-know-what coming and my student-teaching this fall, I need to sock away every penny."

He didn't comment right away, then he said, "He could ride back with me, and you and Jordie could come pick him up on the weekend."

Kat blinked at the outrageous suggestion, momentarily forgetting that Jack didn't even like kids. What kind of mother would send her child off with a stranger? Well, he wasn't a stranger to her, but he was to Tag. She could picture Pete's reaction. "We have orthodontists here, Jack. There's a very reputable group that worked on all my halfsiblings. I'm the only kid in the family who missed out. My dad takes all the credit, of course."

Her flippant response apparently fell on deaf ears. "I'll do everything pro bono. Start to finish. By the time he's in high school, he'll have a smile as perfect as Cooper Lindstrom's."

"Why would you offer to do that? Is it because—"

He cut her off. "I was that kid once, Kat. My dad wasn't an advocate of orthodontia unless there were bite issues, and my mother controlled the purse strings. I didn't get my teeth fixed until I was in college. Kids can be brutal. It messes with your head in a way parents don't understand. Let me do this for Tag."

"But you don't even like him."

His scowl was so pissed off—so Mad Jack—she let out a little yip. "If that's what you think, then this morning was an unforgivable indulgence on your part."

She was immediately ashamed. He was right. He might have gotten off on the wrong foot with the boys, but he was a good man. She'd trust him with her life. And Tag's teeth. But the decision didn't rest with her alone.

"Tag's dad would never go for this. He probably wouldn't even let me take Tag to Denver for an initial consultation. You should have heard the unflattering things he had to say about you after you dropped me off that morning. You're an outsider."

"And I'm obviously interested in you."

She nodded. "That's part of it. Pete's like my dad in that way. He doesn't want me, but he can't stand the idea of someone else in my life, either."

Jack shrugged his broad, solidly made shoulders. "Tough. He doesn't have a say in that. I am involved and I'm not going to disappear." He started to say something else, but instead, pulled out his phone. "What's his number?"

Kat's jaw dropped. "You've got to be kidding."

He waited.

She put her hand flat to her belly. This time was bound to come eventually, she thought. She rattled off Pete's cell number and waited to hear what was said, but Jack stepped away to conduct his conversation in private.

Peeved, she started after him, but was stopped when a small body barreled into her. "Mommy, Mommy, look what Tag stole from that man's motorcycle."

Jordie pointed at Jack, who was looking their way with a grim expression on his face.

Kat sank down and pulled her younger son into her arms. "It was a gift from Jack. Your brother doesn't steal."

"Told ya," Tag said, sticking out his tongue. He and Char walked up. Tag was already wearing his new shirt, although Kat could see the purple neckline of his other shirt under it.

She helped Jordie try on his new shirt, too. The size was right, age-wise, but it was still a little big. He ran his fingers across the logo, which showed a skull where the headlamp should have been on a stylized motorcycle emerging from a blazing inferno. "Wow," he uttered, looking at Char to get her reaction.

"Cool," she said, giving him a high five.

Jack joined them a few seconds later and both boys thanked him for the gifts without Kat's prompting. He seemed pleased by their reactions, but he looked at Kat and said, "He's going to meet me in half an hour at the bar where you were working when I first got to town."

Kat was too stunned to respond until Tag nudged her, a questioning look in his eyes. Kat smiled and ruffled his hair in a way he hated. "I need to go with Jack for an hour or so. It's business. Do you think you could hang out with Char and keep an eye on Jordie? They're going to be serving lunch pretty soon."

Tag looked from Kat to Jack and back. "I guess so."

Kat cleared things with Char, then waited while Jack gave her his cell number. "We'll be back ASAP," he said, flashing a small insider smile Kat's way. "I still have a long drive ahead today."

Kat knew that. She wasn't going to forget it. Men made big promises—to love, honor, forsaking all others as long as you both shall live—then they left women like her and her mother.

She and Jack didn't talk the whole way to Deadwood. Kat was oddly content to lean against his broad back and hold on. She didn't want to think about all of the pressing personal issues on her slate, so she focused on her mother, instead. She'd talked to her aunt earlier. Mom was doing better. Medication was lifting her spirits. Kat was relieved, but she still felt guilty for not getting to Spearfish to see her. She hadn't even introduced her to Jack. And now, it was too late.

She looked up and let the wind steal her sigh. Next week. Hopefully she'd have time after the filming to take the boys for a visit. She had no idea what the job involved, but she was sure she could handle playing an extra.

She was a natural. She'd been an extra all her life.

PETE WAS SITTING at the bar when they arrived. Guy was behind the bar, as usual. He acknowledged her with an understated nod. "Hey, Kat, thought you'd be at the movie-star party. Did you hear they're going to do some filming out front?"

From what the publicist who'd cornered her first thing that morning had said, the film crew was going to be all over the Black Hills taking footage that could be edited into a final cut. "Great for business, huh?"

"Hope so. What can I get you?"

"Water would be good. Guy, have you met Jack?"

"You're Brian's friend, right?"

The two shook hands. "I'm Kat's friend."

Guy glanced at Pete, then back. "O-kay. Beer?"

Jack shook his head. "Another time. Thanks." He looked at Pete and said, "I'll get us a table."

Pete scowled. Kat knew her ex hated to be bossed around. She took her glass of water and followed Jack. After some mostly indistinguishable grumbling, Pete joined them. He set his half-finished draft on the table, then flipped the chair around backward and straddled it. "So, what's this about you being a dentist and wanting to help my kid? Seems pretty obvious you already helped yourself to my ex."

Kat couldn't prevent the blush, but a swift kick to his shin helped alleviate some of her embarrassment.

Pete ignored her. "You're the same guy who was getting a tat the day I picked up Tag, aren't you? Tag said you weren't too friendly."

"Would you let some kid you never met before climb on your twenty-thousand-dollar bike?"

The answer sounded more like Mad Jack than her Jack, but it apparently made sense to Pete. "He should know better. His mom lets him get away with too much."

Kat closed her eyes and sighed. She'd known Pete would get around to assigning blame sooner or later.

"He's a kid," Jack said firmly. "I could have handled things better, but I haven't been around kids much." He shrugged. "Anyway, here's the thing. I asked Kat to marry me."

She jolted upright, completely not expecting that revelation. "And I said no," she quickly inserted.

"I hope to change her mind in the near future. But

the point is I plan to be around your son and Jordie for a long time to come. If the tables were reversed, I'd want to know who was hanging out with my kid."

Pete looked at Kat and said, "You're knocked up."

She tried to bluff. "Didn't you hear what I said? When he asked me to marry him, I said no."

She could see that confused Pete. And Pete hated to be confused. He liked things nice and simple, black and white.

Her brief sense of dodging a bullet—at least temporarily—ended when Jack's eyes narrowed and his gaze locked with hers, but instead of outing her, he said, "About your son's teeth. I'll tell you straight out I specialize in adult orthodontia, but even *I* can tell he's going to need braces. And the sooner you get started, the easier it's going to be on him."

"And you're volunteering to fix his teeth out of the goodness of your heart," Pete said snidely.

Jack's jaw muscle tightened. "I'm volunteering to absorb the cost—whether I do the work or you take him to someone else—because his mother can't afford to have her son's teeth fixed on the paltry amount of child support you pay her."

"Are you saying I'm cheap?"

"Yeah, I am."

Both men jumped to their feet and sort of scratched the ground like a couple of young bull bison trying to impress the dominant female. The thought made her laugh out loud.

They turned to look at her. "I just realized that I'm the matriarch of this tribe," she said, "And I've been doing a pretty damn good job despite the lack of support from my ex-husbands."

She pointed her finger at Pete. "We're changing the amount of child support you pay. Tag couldn't do Little League because I couldn't afford all the driving. That's plain wrong." His scowl looked so much like her father's she almost lost her nerve, but she made herself go on. "Which reminds me. Why am I providing round-trip taxi service to your house? From now on, we pick a half-way point to meet."

"What are you talking about? I was at your place twice last week."

"Oooh. You swung what? Five, six miles out of your way to take your son camping? That was really big of you, Pete."

He had the grace to blush.

"And another thing. No more just dropping him off when you run into some problem with your wife and other kids. That hurts Tag. He may not show it, but it does. It hurt *me* when my parents treated me like a bag of produce."

Pete looked ready to argue, but Jack stepped to her side and put a very large, solid hand on her shoulder. He didn't say anything. He didn't need to. Pete got the message.

"Fine. I'll tell Michelle that as long as we don't have to pay for his teeth out of pocket, the money can go to child support. Within reason," he added, giving Kat a meaningful squint.

She was too riled up to be reasonable. She'd been rea-sonable all her life, and frankly, unreasonable was a lot more empowering. But before she could unload any of the thousand or so long-held complaints she had, Jack said, "You can start by taking Tag while Kat's working as an extra for the TV show. She shouldn't have to scramble to pay for child care when your wife is a stay-at-home mom and you have a pool in your backyard."

Pete gave Kat another black look, but he muttered, "Fine."

Kat wasn't sure exactly what got settled, but neither man seemed inclined toward chitchat, so she and Jack promptly left. As they approached his bike, he said, "I'm sorry if I came on too strong in there. You're more than capable of speaking for yourself, but I noticed with my sister that divorce seems to bring out the worst in people. My ex-brother-in-law got incredibly petty over the dumbest things."

"It's okay. Pete has control issues where women are concerned. It was the main reason behind our divorce. His current wife takes a lot more than I was willing to put up with."

Jack handed her the extra helmet, but she didn't put it on right away. "Just for the record, what are your plans?"

"I'm going back to Denver to start the process of moving."

"What? You're moving here? Seriously?"

"Would you find that easier to believe if I told you I put a down payment on a three-bedroom house in Sentinel Pass today? Well…a small one. I didn't have my checkbook. And it's contingent on a walk-through. I've only seen the place from the outside."

Her jaw dropped. "There aren't any hou— Oh, my God. Mrs. Smith's place? That's where Cooper and Shane are staying."

"Past tense. Coop and Libby are keeping her house, and Shane is at Jenna's. Some crew members are renting it this week. That's why we didn't go inside. But Mrs. Smith's son and daughter were in town to put it on the market, and I made them an offer. They took it."

She shook her head, trying to process this twist. "Jack, we don't even know for sure if I'm pregnant. I haven't taken the test yet. You can't turn your life upside down over this. What if I'm wrong?"

His smile made her heart do a double flip. "Then we have to keep trying till we get it right."

"Jack," she said in her most fervent mother-knows-best tone, "that doesn't make any sense. You barely know me. You're not in love with me. You can't be."

His arm snaked out and he raked her flush against his body. "I know everything I need to know, Kat. I just need to convince you of that. And I can't do that from Denver." He kissed her lightly. "Maybe we could start with a date. You know—the thing two people who are interested in each other do to get to know each other better?"

His grin packed about a thousand watts of swoo, and Kat had trouble remembering what she was going to say. "But…but what about your business?"

"My dad used to preach about the importance of building up a practice and developing strong client relationships, but I watched those valued clients flee like rats from a sinking ship at the first hint of rumors that were patently untrue. Dentistry is my career, not my calling. And certainly not my life. I don't think I realized that until…"

He didn't finish. If he'd said, "until I met you," she wouldn't have believed him, so she didn't press for details. Her head was spinning, and at the moment all she wanted was to get back to her sons. "We should go."

He nodded in agreement and stepped away, reaching into his pocket for the key. "If you don't mind, I think I'll drop you off in Sentinel Pass and keep driving. I want to make Edgemont before dark and I have a bunch of calls to make. But tell Tag I'll be back as soon as I can. If you want to get the ball rolling with a local orthodontist, no problem. Just tell him I plan to consult on the case and send the bill to me."

She yanked on her chin strap. She couldn't think. Her mother liked to say, "The proof was in the pudding." If this talk of moving panned out, fine. She'd deal with him the same way she did Pete and Drew. If he never came back…well, she'd do what she always did. Get by.

CHAPTER FIFTEEN

"You mean you don't even know if there *is* a baby?"

Jack was already tired of this discussion and he'd just started it. He'd waited all week to invite his mother and sister to dinner so he could break the news. Rachel, who'd phoned every evening to check on him, had heard bits and pieces of what had transpired on his journey, but he'd asked her not to tell their mother until he had the majority of his plans finalized.

Fortunately their mother had been playing golf in Grand Junction with a group of retired friends, so he'd been able to conduct most of his business in private. She'd only returned that morning and hadn't questioned his invitation to a Friday-evening barbecue.

"Why doesn't anyone believe me?" he asked, more to himself than either of the women sitting at the table across from him. He'd overcooked the salmon. No one seemed to notice. "I don't care if Kat is pregnant or not. And for the record, she called me on Monday and said she took a home pregnancy test and it was negative. But she still feels pregnant. She's going to give it another week before she sees a doctor."

"Why would this Kat woman say she was pregnant if she didn't know for sure? That sounds terribly irresponsible, Jackson."

"Mom, I think you're missing the point. What Jack is saying is he loves Kat, which is short for Katherine, I believe, and wants to marry her no matter what."

Jack smiled his appreciation. He could tell by the haunted look in his sister's eyes that any talk of love was a painful reminder of her broken heart. Her whirlwind affair and tumultuous marriage had ended so badly she'd barely been able to get out of bed for a month.

"Don't be ridiculous, Rachel. This is Jackson we're talking about. He isn't some flighty character in a romance novel. He's deliberate and intelligent. He makes thoughtful, balanced decisions based on facts and realistic projections."

Jack and his sister exchanged a look. "No, Mom, that's you," Jack said as gently as possible. "I'm more like Dad. I've been trying really hard most of my life not to be because we all know how badly he got burned. But I can't fake it anymore. What happened to Dad was unfortunate. It nearly killed him and left you so jaded about people you forgot Dad's purpose for being a dentist—to help people. Especially children.

"And whether you meant to or not, your fears affected me and my choices. But not anymore. I'm going to work on kids and at least half my practice will be offered free or at reduced prices for people who normally wouldn't be able to afford to take their kids to an orthodontist."

All the color drained from his mother's still-youthful-looking face. Her reddish brown hair lacked even a hint of silver, thanks to her well-paid stylist. "Please tell me you're joking. That's exactly the kind of people who try to take advantage of the system. The boy who accused your father had been coached by his drug-addict parents.

By the time he recanted his statement, it was too late. Both your father—and his practice—were devastated. Neither was ever the same again."

"I know, Mom. But Dad took shortcuts when he was doing pro bono work. He didn't keep a nurse in the room with him. I assume that was because her wages would have been out-of-pocket."

He watched her face change. She didn't deny the fact, which Jack had only guessed. He'd spent most of his drive home from the Hills trying to remember what little he knew about his father's case. There had been a lot of whispers and closed-door conferences with lawyers and investigators. He'd felt his father's shame, and even though Jack never wanted to admit it, he'd had moments of doubt. What if the reason his father didn't have a nurse present was because he'd planned to do something unsavory all along?

But somewhere around Cheyenne another thought had hit him. His trusting father would have tried to honor his own need to help children while conceding to his banker wife's penny-pinching thriftiness.

"Paying staff to fix the teeth of a child who would probably wind up doing drugs or rotting in jail like his father seemed a waste of good money," his mother admitted. "I didn't know how low some people would sink to take advantage of a kind soul. I just didn't know."

Jack wondered how much his mother's sense of guilt had shaped his later decisions, like specializing in adult orthodontics and never dating women with children.

"Mom," Jack said, touching her arm. "Nobody's blaming you. Those were bad people. Dad didn't deserve what happened, but there's no changing the past and I'm tired of letting fear rule my life."

"Jackson, please don't—"

"I'm moving to an area that can't support my tiny window of specialization, Mom. I need to get back into mainstream dentistry, and that means working with children."

"How'd you do it?" Rachel asked. "How'd you overcome your fear?"

Jack looked at her. He heard something deeply personal in her question. He answered honestly, knowing full well neither Rachel nor Mom would understand. "I simply asked myself, 'What would Mad Jack do?'"

Rachel smiled as though she did get it.

His mother let out a low moan. "But what about your beautiful house? The market is soft right now, Jackson. You'll never get what it's worth."

"I'll make money on it no matter what, Mom. And I'm keeping the office building. My colleagues are delighted to continue with our present arrangement. Actually they were thrilled because my not being there means one more piece of the client pie."

He got up and walked around the table. "Mom, Sentinel Pass isn't that far from Denver. I was talking to Kat's friend Libby the other day. Her brother, Mac, makes the drive here about once a month for parts for his mining operation."

Rachel perked up. "Sentinel Pass? Isn't that where the new television show is being filmed? Wow. That's cool. Could you introduce me to a movie star?"

He rolled his eyes. "The only one I met is married to Kat's best friend, but who knows? You can visit me anytime. I'm thinking about building a guest cottage on the property once I finish remodeling the main house and put in a pool."

His mother moaned again. He knew she was thinking about the cost, but what she didn't understand was he'd spend every cent he had to win the heart of the woman he loved.

KAT HELD ON to the counter of Libby's bathroom vanity with her free hand. Her knees felt as if they might give out. Probably because her heart was barely beating and she was breathing too fast and shallowly.

How could this be? she asked herself for the hundredth time, staring at the little plastic wand of the home pregnancy test.

A knock sounded on the door. "Well?" Libby hollered. "What's the verdict? Yea or nay?"

She'd used her mother as an excuse to leave Cooper's big party early on Sunday to drive to Spearfish. A quick stop at the grocery store for *ice cream* had allowed her to pick up a testing kit. And later that night after visiting Mom, who brightened considerably seeing her grandsons, Kat had followed the directions to the letter.

The result had left her baffled. Was there such a thing as a false negative? Could her kit have been old or defective? Maybe she'd tried too soon.

She'd fretted about whether to call Jack, since she still felt pregnant, regardless of what the test said. When she'd finally called him, his reaction had only added to her confusion. How could anybody be that calm and understanding about something so life-altering? He had to be faking all that sweet concern for her state of mind.

But why would he? She didn't get it. Nothing about Jack made sense. Mad Jack she got. He was like all the other men in her life—take what you want and move on. But her Jack? He might be gone, but he rarely left her mind.

And that had scared her more than she wanted to admit. If she wasn't pregnant, then any connection she had with Jack would be lost.

So what? A voice in her head had cried. But the answer wasn't simple. It had grown in strength all week. And by the time Libby had shown up on the set an hour earlier, Kat had been sitting on the curb like a mindless zombie.

Libby had managed to pry out the truth in a matter of seconds. Then, in a bossy but loving way, had insisted on purchasing a second test for Kat to take while the crew was on break. "You have to find out, Kat. It's not fair to you or Jack to drag this out."

Kat opened the bathroom door. "It's negative, too," she said simply.

Libby checked the plastic wand for herself, then nodded. "You're right. It is. I guess that means you're not pregnant. These things are pretty accurate, you know."

"But what about my symptoms? I never miss a period. Never. And my breasts are tender. And I'm queasy all the time—not just in the morning. How do you explain that?"

Libby put her hand on Kat's arm and gently pulled her into the hall. "Let's have a glass of iced tea and talk."

Kat shook her head. "Shane wanted all the extras back on the set in half an hour."

"I'll give you a written excuse," Libby said dryly.

"Besides, half an hour in Shane time could mean three hours on the clock."

They'd already discussed at length the crazy way a television production operated. Despite Shane's passion for schedules, the actual filming seemed dependent on any one of a dozen variables—lighting, wind, the right electrical cords, hair and makeup. Kat wasn't entirely convinced anything got done.

Not that the result mattered to her. Getting paid to do nothing wasn't such a bad thing. She'd managed to find an out-of-the-way corner to work on the last paper she had to turn in for her independent-study class. She'd chosen to write about frontier women in support roles that truly helped to settle the West. Women like Mad Jack's schoolmarm in her dream.

"Kat?"

Kat startled, realizing she'd missed whatever Libby had been saying. "See? Look how ditzy I am. This is me pregnant, Lib. Seriously. Pete used to get so mad at me when he was talking to me and I'd space out."

Libby sat on the rocking chair she always chose when they had book club at her house. Kat perched on the edge of the sofa, restless and a little dazed. She wasn't sure what this meant or what she should do next. Carry on with her life, she supposed. But what about Jack, who was supposedly moving to Sentinel Pass because he thought she was pregnant? She'd messed everything up. Worse than usual.

"Pete has control issues. Forget Pete. Thanks to Jack, he's finally living up to some of his parenting obligations, instead of blaming you every time Tag does something remotely wrong."

In the five days that Jack had been gone, Tag had spent the majority of the time at Pete's house. There was a certain amount of complaining on both parties' part, but Kat was beginning to think Jack—who claimed to know nothing about kids—was more intuitive than she.

"So? Do you want to talk about this false pregnancy?"

"Not really. I feel stupid. And a little betrayed. I mean, I know my body. I can't understand how I got this wrong. Maybe I should see a doctor. There might be something really wrong with me. My mom has cancer, you know."

Libby made a face. "Whoa. No quantum leaps allowed. You're young and healthy. Your mother's throat cancer was the result of a lifetime of bad habits. I think if you'd step back and take stock of your life at the moment, you'd see that any change in your body could be attributed to stress."

"When is my life not stressful, Lib?"

"Good point. But it got more so when Jack showed up."

"Because of his swoo?"

"Because you care for him. Actually I think you love him, but you won't let yourself admit how you feel."

Kat shook her head. She fought the impulse to spring to her feet and start pacing. "I can't love him, Libby. It wouldn't be good for him. I've screwed up every romantic relationship I've ever been in. Jack just had his heart broken. He deserves someone more stable." Like the schoolmarm in her dream.

"Oh, I see. You're not the person he could or should love, so at a deeply subconscious level your body convinces you you're pregnant so he'll marry you?"

Kat stopped fidgeting. In a way, that made sense. But then she remembered. "I turned him down when he asked."

"But maybe a part of you is hoping he won't take no for an answer. Maybe the part that still feels pregnant. Because you don't believe anybody could love you and want to marry you without an ulterior motive."

"Like the threat of my dad's shotgun." Kat's stomach turned over.

Libby sat forward and pounded her fist on her knee. "We all have to deal with baggage from our past, Kat, but I'd wring your father's neck if I had the chance. You've got to start believing that you're not your mother. Or your father. You're you, Kat. One of the nicest, most loving decent people in the world, and I'm sick of you being less than kind to yourself."

Kat couldn't help but smile at her friend's passionate outburst.

Libby sighed heavily but smiled, too. "Kat. Why wouldn't Jack love you? He's smart, and he knows you're exactly what he needs. Why can't you see that?"

Kat pictured herself huddled in the backseat of her mother's car—fingers pushed deep in her ears to block the hurtful words of her parents' shouting matches. How could two people who claimed to be so much in love they didn't even stop to think about birth control wind up hating each other—and the child they made—so much?

She stood. "I need to talk to my dad."

She would have preferred to pose her question to her mother, but her last visit had confirmed Kat's suspicion that her sweet but nosy aunt didn't take a hint well. There was no such thing as privacy with Roberta around.

"What about the boys?"

Kat slapped her brow with the heel of her hand.

"Another brain fart, as Jordie would say. Michelle was supposed to drop Tag off at the Y today to hang out with Jordie after his summer art program. I'll pick them both up on my way to the ranch."

"I could watch them if you want to talk to your dad alone." Libby smiled that loving, happy smile she always got on her face when thinking about her husband. "Cooper loves playing daddy. He won't admit it, but I think he really, really wants a boy." She put her hand on her rounded belly.

"Thanks, Lib. I appreciate the offer—and everything else, too. But the boys have been bugging me about seeing the bison. They can take the four-wheeler out and do a head count while Dad and I talk."

Not that she was expecting any huge breakthroughs. Her father wasn't all that self-aware, although he was good at assigning blame. Talking to him might be a mistake, but she needed to find out why her body had tricked her into believing something that wasn't true.

Then she had to call Jack. She felt terrible about inadvertently creating this stupid firestorm. He'd probably lose a whole bunch of money by backing out of his purchase of the Smith house. And who knew what else he'd done to start the ball rolling?

She didn't know how he would take the news. Would he be angry? Or relieved? The two prime emotions Pete and Drew would have displayed—most vocally. But Jack was an enigma.

Tomorrow. She'd call him in the morning and that would be that.

CHAPTER SIXTEEN

AN EMPTY JACK DANIEL'S bottle in the trash wasn't a good omen, Kat thought as she passed through the kitchen of the log home she'd always loved. The place seemed pretty tidy, though. Not the way it had when her father was on a bender and she was expected to keep it clean.

She called out his name but didn't get an answer, so she headed toward his bedroom at the back of the house. It wasn't unusual for him to take a late-afternoon "nap" on days that began with a cocktail for breakfast.

After a quick stop at home to change into her jeans and boots and grab a few things for the boys, she'd driven into Rapid to pick them up. Shane had thoughtfully cut every one of the extras a check after they'd wrapped up filming. Hers included a nice little bonus for providing henna tattoos to the wives and girlfriends of the staff who'd traveled from California for the week.

Jenna had suggested the idea when Kat had complained about being bored the first day of filming. The tattooing had been a nice diversion on Monday and Tuesday. After that, Kat had used the downtime to study. Two fewer worries that might have added to her stress— her paper was done *and* her car had a full tank.

She paused to glance out the window. Even through the thick log walls she could hear the tinny rattle of the old quad her father let the boys drive. "Find the herd and take an accurate head count," she'd told them. "But don't hop the fence. This is rutting season and the young bulls are very unpredictable. Got it?"

Tag had heaved his old-man sigh while Jordie had jumped up and down with excitement. She wasn't sure her younger son understood what rutting meant, but no doubt his world-weary older brother would explain if the opportunity to point out the act arose.

She shuddered with resignation and walked the rest of the way down the hall. "Dad?" She knocked lightly on his bedroom door.

She didn't enter until he answered, "Huh? Kat? Is that you?"

She opened the door, her heart climbing into her throat. To her surprise, he wasn't stretched out in bed, rumpled and bleary-eyed. He was seated at his desk. His computer was on and a stack of bills rested beside the keyboard. "Am I interrupting?"

He pushed himself back and stood. "A welcome break. Is that the quad I hear? You musta brought my grandsons along."

She came a little closer, still not trusting the clear look in his eyes. Maybe he only had a little nip before the bottle ran out, she thought. "They're going to find the bison. Is that okay? They haven't been here for a while and I—"

"Of course, it's fine. I figured Jordie was probably going through bison withdrawals about now. He does love the big woollies."

Her heart twisted oddly. She hadn't realized her father was so observant. "I know. He's a softie. Like me."

Buck's bushy left eyebrow rose. "I wouldn't say that. You can be as prickly as any one of those rosebushes in the garden. And you're as tough as nails when it comes to keeping your boys in line."

She blinked. Was that a compliment? It almost sounded like one. "What's going on, Dad? Are you loaded? You don't look drunk, but free compliments? That's not like you."

She waited for an explosion, but instead of blowing up at her remarks, he laughed. "You got that right. I ain't saying otherwise. But fact is, that bottle you probably spotted in the trash is the last of my hidden stash. I'd forgotten I planted it in the tack room. Emptied the whole thing down the sink."

He seemed sincere, but she wasn't buying it. "I've been after you for years to stop drinking. Why now?"

He shook his head. "I don't know. It's not like I found God or learned I have cancer or anything. I just woke up one morning with a bad hangover and told myself this is a stupid way to waste what's left of my life. I called a friend of mine who goes to AA and he picked me up for a meeting."

"You're going to AA?"

He made a wobbly motion with his hand. "Joining things isn't my way, but I know they're there if I need a little help. And Ray, my buddy, says I can always call him."

She didn't know what to say, but the fact that he was lucid and in a fairly good mood might actually work in her favor. "Want a cup of coffee?" he asked.

She started to say no. She avoided caffeine when she

was pregnant. But then she remembered the test she'd taken at Libby's. "Okay."

She followed him to the kitchen and hopped up on a stool at the counter. "Dad, I wanted to talk to you about you and Mom. Your marriage."

He groaned. "What for? That's old news."

"But I've made the same mistake. Twice. And now Jack's asked me to marry him. I don't want to blow it again."

"Are you knocked up?"

She stuck her tongue out at his back. "No, I'm not." She couldn't believe how much satisfaction it gave her to say that—even though she still felt most of the symptoms that had convinced her she was pregnant. And she still hadn't gotten her period, either.

"Then why the hell do you want to get married?"

She let him finish filling the carafe before answering. "I didn't say I did. But he's buying a house in Sentinel Pass and moving his practice up here from Denver. He doesn't seem to want to take no for an answer. Why? I really have no idea."

Buck chuckled softly. "No. I don't suppose you do."

"What's that mean?" she bristled. "That I'm so unlovable only a man who got me pregnant first would want to marry me?"

His eyes narrowed in a way that used to scare her to death. She crossed her arms and didn't look away. He took a step closer. Her heart sped up. The little kid in her was ready to pee her pants, but she clenched her jaw and waited.

"If your mother and I made you feel unlovable, Katherine, I'm sorry."

Katherine. The name sounded funny coming from his lips. Formal, yet tender. Respectful, even. Her jaw dropped. "Really?"

He nodded. "That's what you want to know, isn't it? Why we fought so much? Why you got caught in the crossfire? I'm not stupid. I know you felt like you were to blame most of the time, but it wasn't you, honey girl. I'm an ornery old cuss who doesn't like to admit when he's wrong. I was wrong a lot when I was married to your mother. I loved her more than any woman ever, but we couldn't be alone in a room without either making love or trying to kill each other. It might be some weird chemistry. I don't know."

Kat truly hadn't expected his honesty. Or frankness. "You guys fought about me all the time, but then when I came here to stay with you, you ignored me."

His face screwed up in a sheepish look she couldn't ever remember seeing. "I didn't know squat about raising a little girl, but I was afraid if I let your mother have you all the time, she'd convince you I didn't want you."

"You did? Want me?"

"Hell, yes. Why do you think I helped you buy those damn bison? You know we've never made a dime on them, and I could have fattened a couple thousand head of cattle on the grass they eat. But I kept 'em. Because they were yours and you love them and I...well, you know."

Even now he couldn't say the words, but she understood. He loved her. He'd always loved her. He just didn't know how to show it. Except where her herd was concerned.

The revelation left her a little dizzy. Maybe coffee

wasn't such a good idea. She might spin right off into the sky like a dust devil.

And what any of this meant to her relationship with Jack, she didn't have a clue.

She thought about asking her father for advice—maybe this new touchy-feely Buck could offer her some insights into how to handle a crazy man who was poised to turn his life upside down for nothing. But just as she opened her mouth to speak, the high-pitched pinging sound of a quad engine revved at full bore came in through the window.

Buck turned and looked outside. "Uh-oh."

She was out the door and down the steps before the four-wheeler entered the yard. Tag was driving, his thin body hunched forward as if willing the quad to go faster. Jordie's arms were clenched around his brother's middle, but she couldn't see any more than the crown of his helmet.

Something was wrong. Her maternal instinct told her that. She just didn't know what. Had the bike hit a bump and Jordie got tossed off? Their helmets were hand-me-downs and probably not as good as they should be. She'd never forgive herself if—

"Mom, it wasn't my fault," Tag said, turning off the ignition as the quad rolled to a stop. He hopped to the ground, gesturing excitedly. "I told him to stay on this side of the fence, but he saw a baby by itself. No mother bison around. Jordie thought it might be hurt or caught in wire or something. He wasn't even halfway between me and the bison when this young bull came out of nowhere and charged him. Jordie's fast, Mom. He would have made it fine if he hadn't tripped."

By now Kat was at the vehicle. Her fingers lightly skimmed over her son's back and chest, but he continued to keep his hands locked across the lower half of his face.

"Did the bull stomp him?" Buck asked. "You point out which one it was and I'll shoot the mo—it…dead on the spot."

Jordie's eyes went wide and he let out a muffled cry.

"The bull never touched him, Grandpa. You know they don't see that good, and once Jordie was on the ground the bull veered off in the other direction."

"What happened to your mouth, honey? Can I see?"

He shook his head.

"I think he broke some teeth, Mom."

Kat looked at her youngest son's eyes. Tear tracks had left grayish streaks in the dust on his pudgy cheeks. His muffled sniffling and constant blinking told her he was ready to burst into tears again.

"It's okay, sweetie. Accidents happen. Don't cry." She scooped him off the seat and into her arms. He looped his arms around her neck and buried his face in her neck as she carried him to the porch. His tears came in earnest and within seconds he was wailing.

"Don't worry, Jordie boy. Let Mommy see." She sat on the top step and settled him on her knee. She gently pried his hands away, trying not to let the sight of blood and dirt around his mouth influence her already queasy stomach. "There's so much dirt I can't really see. Dad, could you get us a glass of water?"

Buck was already charging into the house as she continued to comfort her son. "Don't make yourself sick crying, Jordie. It'll be okay. I promise."

How? a little voice asked. Every penny she'd earned this summer was spoken for once she started student-teaching.

She carefully loosened the chin strap of the helmet and eased it over his ears. His hair was damp with sweat and stuck up in spiky clumps.

"I brought some ice, in case there's swelling," her father said, joining her on the step. He laid a towel across her knee and set a plastic bag of ice beside her foot. Pulling Jordie a little closer, he bent down to take a look. "Open up, kiddo," he coaxed in the gentlest voice Kat had ever heard.

Eyes squeezed tight, Jordie clenched his fists and slowly opened his mouth. His tongue looked gritty. "Yuck!" Tag cried. "You really did eat dirt."

Jordie's tears started again. Kat gave her older son a severe look. She was just reaching for the glass of water Buck had set beside the ice when her dad jumped to his feet. "Here. Wait. This will work better," he said.

He grabbed a nearby hose and turned the water on low. Jordie tried to bolt, but Kat said firmly, "We have to see, honey. You can do this. Lean over the step and rinse and spit. Good idea, Dad."

It took three tries to get his mouth clear enough for a good look at the damage. His front two teeth had been bent all the way back, exposing their little roots. The tooth just left of the middle stuck sideways like a piece of jagged glass. It was broken and seemed to have punctured the inside of his cheek. A couple of other teeth looked loose, but Jordie wouldn't let her touch them.

"What a mess," her father declared, which made Jordie start to cry again.

"Dad," Kat complained. "It's not that bad, honey. We'll call a dentist and see if we can get you in right away."

"On a Friday night? In August?" the Buck of old said in disgust.

Her father was right, but she couldn't just sit there and wait until Monday. "There must be someone we can call in an emergency."

"How 'bout Jack?" Tag asked.

Kat looked at Jordie, who nodded. "J'k," he said, the word whistling through the gap in his teeth.

"Too bad Jack's in Denver,' she muttered.

Denver. A drive she could make in seven or eight hours if she left now.

Her father straightened and reached into his pocket. He held out a key ring. "Take mine. It's got a full tank of gas and there's room for the boys to stretch out in the back. Plus, I won't have to worry about you breaking down. It's got a built-in phone and you can let me know when you get there."

Her car was a compact. It got better mileage. But it was also old. And needed the radiator flushed. Buck's SUV was brand-new. Kat had never even been in it. Her hand was shaking as she reached for the keys. "Are you sure?"

When she looked at her father, she was almost certain she saw a hint of tears in his eyes. But he turned away before she could be sure. "Load up the boys. I'll pack you a lunch so you don't have to stop."

She closed her fingers around the fancy key ring. She could do this. For Jordie.

"STOP PACING."

"I can't. If you don't like it, go home."

"No. I want to meet her. And you might need me."

Jack looked at his sister. "You're not a dental assistant."

"I know. But when I was, like, fifteen or sixteen, Dad used to pay me to come in on Saturdays to do some filing and help out. He wasn't very busy by then, but I learned a little bit. At the very least, I could be a witness."

He swirled to face her. "Don't tell me Mom got to you during dinner. Kat is not an opportunist. She hasn't been coaching her son to screw me over. She isn't like that, Rachel."

"If you say so, but why risk it? I'll be your assistant and everybody's happy."

He was sorry he'd checked his answering machine from her house. He'd walked her home after their mother left so they could talk about her life, which she felt was going nowhere since her divorce. She'd been standing close enough to overhear Kat's frantic voice message. And she'd listened just as attentively when Jack called back.

Jordie was hurt. A couple of broken teeth. She needed Jack to look at him and tell her what to do.

Jack was touched that she trusted him enough to call. And here was a chance to put his new plan into effect. If he couldn't handle sweet little Jordie, he couldn't be a regular dentist.

He'd given Kat directions to his house. If Jordie's teeth needed immediate attention, they'd go to the office. Apparently with his sister at his side.

The flash of headlights in his driveway set them both into motion. Rachel opened the door and let Jack lead the way to the unfamiliar SUV that was idling a few feet away. The inside dome light was on, so Jack could see Kat behind the wheel. She'd turned to face the backseat. The rear windows were tinted, so Jack couldn't see any movement.

He rapped lightly on the passenger window. It disappeared quietly into the door. "Hi," he said. "You made great time."

"Luck and lack of traffic," she said. Her gaze shifted to the person behind him.

"This is my pesky sister, Rachel. I was at her house when you called and she thinks she can be of some help, although I doubt it."

Rachel bumped him from behind to reach out to Kat. "Hi. Sorry to meet you under these circumstances. How's your little boy?"

Kat shook Rachel's hand, but Jack could tell she was frazzled and the only thing on her mind was Jordie. "He's asleep," she said in a low whisper. "I took your advice and stopped at home for his pillow and favorite blanket and I gave him some children's painkiller."

Jack poked his head inside the car and looked in the backseat. His heart twisted. Beneath the jumble of pillows and blankets, Jordie was curled up beside his older brother, whose arm was around the younger boy protectively. If he'd ever worried that he couldn't love these children, his fear vanished in an instant, and he felt a powerful need to protect them and care for them.

"Instead of waking him here, then moving to the office, why don't we just head over there now? If Tag doesn't wake up when we move Jordie, Rachel can wait in the car with him."

"I'm awake, Mom," Tag said softly. "Jordie's breath stinks, but I didn't want to move him."

Kat smiled for the first time, and Jack had no trouble reading the depth of love she felt for her older son.

Jack opened the passenger door and got in. To his sister, he said, "Follow us."

Her Porsche Boxter was parked behind the third door of his three-stall garage.

"I really appreciate this, Jack," Kat said as she backed out. "You have no idea."

"I think I do. I'm only sorry you had to drive so far. If this had happened a few weeks from now, I would have been closer." He shrugged. "Although then, I might not have had a state-of-the-art dental facility at my disposal. I haven't gotten that far in my relocation plans."

"You know, we really have to talk about that," she started. "I took—"

"We will. Later. Or tomorrow. You're staying at my house tonight, of course. Turn right at the corner."

She made a soft sound of exasperation. "When did you get so bossy?"

"Dr. Treadwell, Mr. Hyde," he said, wishing they had time for a private moment. She looked like a woman who needed a hug and he was just the man to give her one. But this wasn't about them. "Turn left at the next light and move into the far-right lane."

He could see the tiniest glimmer of a smile on her lips, but she didn't say another word until they reached the office. "Pull up to the front door. If the security people come by to check on us, Rachel can deal with them."

Jack hopped out the moment the car came to a stop. He motioned for his sister to park beside the SUV, then he tossed her his key ring. "Go ahead and open up. The code is Mother's birth date. If you tell her that, I'll never whiten your teeth again." He hurried around the car to where Kat was holding the rear passenger door open. She had a confused look on her face, so he explained, "Mom's kind of vain about her age, and everyone who works here has the code. If she thought they knew what it stood for, she'd be royally ticked off."

He could tell Kat was trying to be polite, but her main focus was Jordie. He heard her suck in a breath when Jack bent over and scooped the half-asleep child up in his arms. He turned and kept walking even as Jordie started to fuss. "No, Mommy. I'm fine now. I don't want to see no denith."

His lisp broke Jack's heart.

In his kindest, gentlest tone, he tried to soothe the boy. "This is an old-fashioned dentist office, Jordie. We have balloons and candy for our patients. My dad was a dentist, and he believed that every child who was brave enough to open his mouth to have his teeth checked deserved a reward."

"Candy?" Tag said, his tone skeptical. "I thought candy was bad for your teeth."

"It's sugar-free," Rachel said. She was waiting with the door open. "I turned on the lights in the first exam room, Jack," she said, pointing down a hallway he rarely visited. Cosmetic dentistry was on the second floor.

She locked the door and hurried to catch up. "Do you like Xbox?" she asked Tag.

Jack glanced over his shoulder and saw the look Tag gave her. Half curious, half get-out-of-my-face, crazy lady. God, he loved that kid.

"I played Grand Theft Auto at my friend David's house once. It was pretty cool. You got to run over girls. And the helicopter cut people's heads off."

"Taggart John Linden!" Kat exclaimed. "Tell me you're kidding."

He blanched, obviously forgetting about his mother's presence in his effort to sound cool. "Oh, Mom, it was just the one time. Now his mom keeps the R-rated games locked in her desk."

"Interesting. I've heard of that one, but never tried it," Rachel said. "But I know for a fact that Jack's got Madden. Do you like football?"

Jack could tell Tag was dying to follow Rachel wherever she might lead, but he hesitated, looking to his mother for his cue. "Go ahead, hon. You don't have to be in the exam room with us. But don't play with anything else. And tell Mrs....um...Rachel thank you."

"Just Rachel. I'm nobody's missus."

Jack hated the fatalistic tone he heard in his sister's voice. Rachel was one of the coolest people he knew. She deserved better where love was concerned. So did Kat.

"We'll be in here, Tag," he said, turning to enter the exam room. He carried his patient to the perfectly proportioned chair that was covered in a jungle print. On the ceiling was a mural of monkeys, colorful birds and snakes that looked right out of a Disney movie. Regulars to this office knew that if they pointed out a very tiny Tarzan figure hiding behind one of the trees, they'd get an extra prize at the end of the exam.

Jack handed the blanket that had come with Jordie to Kat. "Are you warm enough?" he asked his patient.

Jordie nodded. As Jack had hoped, his attention was drawn to the colorful display and away from the tray of sterilized tools on the counter behind them. "Have you ever had an X ray of your mouth, Jordie?"

"No," Kat answered, "but he had a checkup last fall in school. He brought home a certificate that said everything looked good and he had no cavities."

Jack pulled on a pair of latex gloves and used his foot to position his stool. He sat so he was eye level with Jordie. "That's great. That means your teeth are strong. But I won't know for sure until I look inside. Can you open up for me?"

Tears glistened in the boy's eyes, but he bravely inched his jaws apart. Jack angled the overhead light to give him a crisp view. He did his best not to let anything show on his face. "Wow. You are one tough kid, Jordie. Did you leave a dent on the rock you hit?"

Jordie grunted mutely.

Jack looked at Kat. In his peripheral vision, he noticed that Rachel had returned. He told them both, "For tonight, I'd like to get some X rays and affix a little sealant to the two broken teeth. They'll probably need to be pulled, but I'd like to save them if possible."

"You mean like a crown? On a baby tooth? Won't that be expensive?" Kat asked.

Before Jack could figure out how to put his answer in a way that wouldn't sound like charity, Rachel said, "Our father had one strict rule. Family was always free. Remember those crazy cousins of Mother's who planned their entire vacation around coming to Denver to get free dental work? Drove Mom nuts," she added.

Jack had no idea what she was talking about, but he nodded gamely and played along. "And how many times did he have to redo Aunt Peggy's bridge? A dozen, at least."

Kat looked from Jack to Rachel and back. He

couldn't tell if she bought the lie or not, but she finally sighed. "I'm not family."

"You will be," Rachel said, patting her back. "I have no doubt about that."

Jack would have hugged her, but he had too many things to do before he lost his patient to boredom, fear or fatigue. Any one of the regular children's dentists in the building could have done things faster and more efficiently, but Jack didn't want to make any mistakes, and he was determined to do his best for Jordie.

Kat watched for as long as she could, but when the stress of the day and the long drive finally caught up with her, she curled up in the chair Rachel had dragged in from the waiting room. She let her head nod into the soft blanket that carried her son's scent and closed her eyes.

She knew in her heart of hearts that Jack was treating her son as if he were his own. Rachel was at Jack's side performing every command her brother made with surprisingly few mistakes, given this wasn't her job. Kat thought she heard Jack say something about counting beans for a living, but mostly she'd tuned out their banter.

Her son was either too scared or too tired to complain about anything Jack did. And Kat was too groggy to follow beyond the basics. They'd all agreed that Jack would fix what he could tonight to make sure there would be no infection and pain. In the morning he'd call one of his colleagues to confirm that Jordie was on the right treatment path. Everything was going to be free.

Kat would have felt like a charity case, but she didn't. She felt…cherished. And special. Jack stepped up and did what needed to be done. The way Mad Jack would have. He was a hero in every sense of the word.

And she loved him. The real Jack. Not her imaginary dream man. But she still couldn't agree to marry him. All her bluster about deserving something better than a man who only wanted to do the right thing by their child was bull. She was a good mother. She was determined to be a dedicated teacher. But she was so lousy at relationships she wouldn't dream of ruining this wonderful man's life by agreeing to marry him.

She simply had to make him wake up and see the reality of their situation before he ruined his perfect life.

CHAPTER SEVENTEEN

"YOU'RE GONNA marry me and that's that."

"I'm not one of those women from the bar, Jack. You can't tell me what to do."

"Hellfire and damnation, woman," he said, throwing his hat on the dusty ground between them. "Has anyone ever told you you're the most pigheaded person this side of the Missouri?"

Katherine continued to rock, the knitting needles in her hands keeping time to the *click* of the chair against the uneven planks of the porch. "I am not. That distinction is reserved for the man who insists on marriage despite the fact he could be shot and leave me a widow on any given day that he puts on that holster."

His steely gray eyes narrowed to that squint so many feared. "People die, Katherine. Not just people who use guns. Your family took sick and left you all alone, but you can't stop living because you don't want to feel that pain again. Pain is what reminds us we're alive. Pain and love."

"Maybe I don't deserve to be alive."

He cleared the distance between them in two long strides and yanked her to her feet. The grip on her wrist stung, but she didn't pull away. She met his angry gaze chin high. "Don't you see? You're alive for a reason. I've had more close calls than you ever want to know about, but I'm here now—with you—because we have a purpose beyond just living out our days. We have a chance to make a family. To bring normal to this wild place."

He let her go, undid his gun belt and let it drop. It landed with a thudding sound nearly as loud as her heartbeat.

"Without you, I will die. It's only a matter of time. My reflexes will slow. A young pup looking to make a name for himself will beat me to the draw. You're my last hope, Katherine. Can't you see that?"

KAT SAT UP in bed, heart racing. She looked around and recognized nothing. She had no idea where she was. Or when. The dream had been so real. She could still taste Jack's kiss. A hint of mint from the leaf he'd picked near her porch. He'd called her his last hope.

"No," she said, shaking her head. She wasn't anybody's hope. She was a lodestone. A burden. No matter how hard she tried to tread lightly in other people's lives, she always managed to screw up. Just ask her two exes.

The Jack in her dreams was poised to give up his way of life for her. The Jack in real life was in the process of throwing away his established business to move closer to her. Talk about utter madness. She didn't get it.

Why me? she wanted to shout at the top of her lungs.

She closed her eyes and took a deep breath. When she opened them, she felt calmer. But she wasn't going anywhere today until she got an answer.

She hopped out of the guest-room bed. She'd been too exhausted to notice much last night. By the time they got back to Jack's house and she'd put the boys to bed, she'd barely had enough energy left to brush her teeth and crawl under the covers.

The room was lovely. The gold- and rust-colored silk spread contained strands of teal that picked up accents in the wall hangings and dried flower arrangement on the Craftsman-style dresser. Everything was so perfect she suspected a designer had had a say in the decor.

After peeking in on the boys, who were crashed on an air bed in the room beside hers, she took a shower and dressed in record speed. The light murmur of a television coming from the first floor let her know that Jack was awake and moving around downstairs.

At least, she hoped the woman's voice she heard was Diane Sawyer and not Jack's sister. While Kat liked Rachel and hoped to see her before she left town—and thank her for her help last night—at the moment she needed some alone time with Jack before the boys woke up.

She followed the sound toward the back of the house. She couldn't help but admire the home's tasteful design, although there were too many breakable art objects on low tables to give the place a kid-friendly feel.

Her flip-flops made a *shush-shush* sound on the terrazzo tile. Jack must have heard her coming because he met her at the doorway. "Kat. You're up. I was hoping you'd be able to sleep in. How are you feeling?"

"Pretty good, thanks."

"I have the water on if you'd like tea."

He didn't move when she stepped closer. Even

though she had every intention of ending things with him today, she was tempted, so very tempted, to throw herself into his arms for a good cry.

Damn hormones. Even if she wasn't pregnant, something was whacked out inside her body. Maybe what she was feeling was swoo whiplash.

"Do you have any juice? Something cold sounds good."

"Pineapple orange?" he asked, ushering her into the kitchen/dining nook, which with its twelve-foot ceilings, arched windows and faux-suede paint job the color of the juice he'd just offered to give her could have appeared on the pages of a decorating magazine.

She froze the second she caught sight of two women seated on the opposite side of the large, U-shaped counter. Their reflections were visible in the shiny perfection of the gold-flecked onyx marble countertop. Rachel and an auburn-hair woman who simply had to be Jack's mother. She looked exactly the same as the photo Kat had found in his wallet.

"Kat, this is my mother, Rosaline. And you remember Rachel, of course."

Kat screwed up her courage. She'd never had a great relationship with either of her mothers-in-law, despite the fact that they were very nice women. She'd always wondered if the circumstances behind the weddings to their sons had put a strain on their relationships from the get-go.

"Good morning," she said, taking a step closer. She wasn't sure if she should offer to shake hands. "Did Rachel tell you what a hero your son is?"

Rosaline's perfectly sculpted eyebrow arched with an air of disdain. "I'm absolutely certain she didn't leave out a single detail. That's all she's talked about all morning."

Kat looked at Rachel, who shrugged good-naturedly. Her mother's waspish tone seemed to drift right past her. Kat was envious. "Oh, Mother, get off your high horse. Jack and I have both told you that Kat is the one. You'd better be nice to her, or you'll never see your future grandchildren. And believe me, Kat's kids are great and you're going to want to know them, too."

Kat was too shocked by Rachel's assumption to respond. Until Jack took her hand and put a cold juice glass in it. She immediately set it down and faced Rachel. "You're jumping to conclusions that aren't based on fact. I came here because Jack is the only dentist I know who might possibly have helped us on a Friday night. Maybe if I'd been thinking straight, I could have called around, but when your child is in pain, all you can think of is how to fix things the fastest."

"So you drove eight hours to Denver," Rachel said, a knowing smile on her lips.

Kat felt her face heat. "I trust him."

Rachel crowed triumphantly. "You love him, Kat. It's okay to admit that."

Kat looked at Jack, who took a deep breath and let it out. His sigh was filled with a frustration that probably went back to the day his parents brought his baby sister home from the hospital. "For someone who has—as recently as yesterday—declared love to be an emotional black hole that sucks all joy and hope from one's soul, you sure seem eager for me and Kat to get together. What's that about?"

"Your sister needs therapy," Jack's mother said.

"She won't admit how unbalanced the divorce left her. She's probably projecting her unfulfilled dreams on the both of you."

Rachel laughed. "Whatever. The point is, Mother, that you and I are in the wrong place at the wrong time, and we're leaving right this instant so Jack and Kat can talk."

When Rosaline started to protest, Rachel shushed her. "That was our deal, remember? You had until Kat woke up to try to convince Jack that he was making a huge mistake." To Kat, she said, "*I* don't think that, but Mother hasn't had a chance to get to know you. Once she does, she'll come around. I was thinking I might lock her in a room with Tag and an Xbox and see what happens. What do you think?"

Kat kept her opinion to herself.

Rachel, who obviously was used to getting her way, hustled her mother out the door with barely a chance for the older woman to voice her protest. Rosaline's last words were, "Call me when your company is gone, Jackson. We need to talk."

Kat echoed the sentiment once the sound of Rachel's sports car's engine faded. "Jack, we need to talk."

"I know, Kat. But first I want to show you something."

His tone reminded her of Jordie when he brought home an art project that spelled MOM in macaroni. "What?" she asked suspiciously.

He stepped closer and turned sideways before carefully rolling back the edge of his loose, short-sleeved Hawaiian shirt.

Her involuntary gasp made her sip of juice lodge sideways in her throat. Tears burned in her eyes as she coughed and sputtered. "You have a tattoo. A real one."

He nodded, stretching his neck to look at it. "I know. See what it says?"

She brushed the tears from her eyes—coughing tears, not real tears—and looked again. Her name in a heart. How cheesy. But knowing how much he feared needles and everything he'd endured with the black ink made her eyes fill with moisture again. Real tears this time.

"It says 'Kat.'"

"Yeah, it does. Thank God you don't go by Katherine." His tone was light, but she knew he wasn't kidding.

"Were you drugged?"

He shook his head. "I had one of my colleagues give me a prescription for a mild tranquilizer, but I didn't fill it. I decided that since I'm asking you to be brave enough to risk marriage again, I needed to get over my old phobias, as well."

She shook her head. "Jack, they're not the same thing. Marriage is a lifetime commitment."

"I know. So is a tattoo."

She smiled. She couldn't help it. "Jack…"

"Kat…"

"You're crazy."

He nodded. "Some might call me mad."

A flutter started in her belly and quickly passed through all her limbs. "What did you say?"

He ran a hand through his hair—longer now than when she'd first met him and speculated about his receding hairline beneath his skull-and-crossbones do-rag. Had he grown into his looks these past weeks or had her perception of him changed?

"I know this is going to sound bizarre, but the first night we were together at the motel, I had this dream where I was a gunslinger named Mad Jack and I swept this beautiful schoolmarm named Katherine off her feet. I was prepared to love her, then get the hell out of Dodge, as they say, but instead, I fell in love with her."

"You? Or Mad Jack?"

He made a face as he pondered the question. "A week ago I would have said Mad Jack. I honestly didn't think I was capable of being someone like that. In charge of my life. Fearless. Independent. Afraid of nothing—not even needles."

"What changed?"

"You made me realize that I could do anything I wanted. Even when I failed—like with the black ink—you didn't judge me. That was really empowering, Kat. And I've seen you do the same with your children. It's what's going to make you a fabulous teacher."

"Really?"

He nodded. "Funny how other people can see things about us that we seem to miss. It took a figment of my subconscious to get over a lifetime of fears. Needles. Kids. Love."

"You were afraid of love?" She was afraid her knees were going to give out.

He led her to the stool his mother had been sitting on. "Afraid to love completely, honestly. Afraid to be vulnerable. I think that's one thing we have in common."

She sat, but her focus was fixed on what he was saying. "I've been vulnerable all my life, Jack. I never take precautions to protect myself. Obviously. I have two children to prove it."

He put his hands on the armrests of the stool and leaned in to kiss her forehead. "Neither of your sons was an accident. They came into your life to fill a void. Just like you came into mine to fill an empty spot where my heart should have been.

"Kat, you have to marry me. I told you about my dream. I've risked your laughing at me—or worse, calling me crazy. I can't bare any more of my soul than that."

Did she dare tell him the truth?

Before she could make up her mind, the sound of voices—her children's voices—filtered through the doorway. She expected Jack to pout about the interruption. Both Pete and Drew would have. Instead, he threw back his head and laughed. "In here, boys," he called in a booming voice. "Who wants pancakes?"

To Kat, he added, "Soft food for Jordie."

That was when she knew the truth. Jack was not a mistake. He was a gift. And only a fool would turn her back on someone fate went to such great lengths to put in her life.

Unfortunately Kat had yet to tell him the truth. She wasn't pregnant. She still hadn't seen a doctor, but two over-the-counter tests seemed to trump her symptoms, which probably were the result of stress, as Libby suggested.

Once he found out about the baby—or rather the lack of a baby—he'd probably rethink his proposal. What man wouldn't? What man in his right mind would marry someone like her? Someone with all her baggage—two ex-husbands, two kids with bad teeth, a crazy, convoluted, completely dysfunctional family and a herd of bison?

Not a single man she could name. Not even Mad Jack.

JACK WAS SHOCKED by how fast the morning shot by. Jordie seemed to rebound from his ordeal with inordinate healing ability. Just a casual check of his mouth showed excellent improvement. Jack had made an appointment for two o'clock with the colleague he'd most trust with his own child. Kat had made calls to her parents, her girlfriends and both boys' fathers to keep them abreast of what was happening. She planned to leave right after the checkup, unless there was some pressing need for action that Jack had missed.

He was sorry their heart-to-heart had been interrupted, but he couldn't blame the boys for wanting to be near their mother. A video game kept Tag occupied, but Jordie had refused to leave Kat's side even for a minute—until Rachel showed up with ice cream and watermelon.

"Outside on the patio, boys," she said, marching through the kitchen like the Pied Piper. "My brother likes a neat house. He'd never condone a seed-spitting contest indoors."

Jack had never seen this side of his sister before and wasn't sure why she was taking such an active interest in two children who may or may not wind up being part of the family. The answer to that question rested with Kat, who had turned him down so often he wasn't sure what to expect.

"We'll be right out," he called after her. "I need to draw Kat a map to get her safely out of town. You know what traffic is like around here."

Rachel rolled her eyes, but the boys seemed to buy the excuse. Even Jordie.

Once the glass door closed behind them, he turned to Kat and said bluntly, "Yes or no? Are you pregnant?"

She winced in a way that made him regret his lack of tack. "The simple answer is no."

"There's a not-so-simple answer?"

"My mind says I'm pregnant. My body acts like I'm pregnant. The home pregnancy tests I've taken say I'm not. I plan to see a doctor next week. Libby thinks it's stress. My aunt said it could be a tumor on the ovary. She used to be a nurse. I called to ask her advice *for a friend*."

The suggestion made his knees weak, but he pulled her into his arms and hugged her tight. "Do you have health insurance?"

She shook her head. "The boys do through their dads, but not me."

He eased back slightly. "All the more reason to get married right away." He kept his tone light, but he was serious and he wanted her to know that.

"I'm not your schoolmarm, Jack. I don't need rescuing."

"Did I say that Mad Jack rescued her?" He shook his head. "He swept her off her feet, but she's the one who saved him. His life—like mine—was going nowhere. She made him look beyond what he knew and take a leap of faith toward a life he wanted but didn't think he deserved. Sound familiar?"

Her teeth caught her bottom lip and she nodded ever so slightly. "You've got that part right. I don't deserve you, Jack."

"Because I'm such a fabulous catch?" he asked incredulously. "You were right about me from the start, Kat. I'm a R.U.B. That's one letter short of a rube. In many circles, I'm a joke. But I'm not as much of a joke as I was before I met you." He pointed to his arm. "I have the tattoo to prove it."

She shook her head. "You're not a joke to me, Jack. I got hit with a serious shot of swoo the moment I saw you."

"I have swoo?"

"Big-time."

"Really? Enough to, say, sweep you off your feet?"

"Yeah."

"And make you agree to marry me?"

She didn't answer right away. "Don't you want to find out what the doctor says first?"

He shook his head. "I don't care what the doctor says, Kat. If there's something wrong, I want to be at your side every step of the way. If the negative sign should have been a plus, then I want to experience every part of our pregnancy."

"Our?"

"Yours, mine, Mad Jack's…"

She laughed, then. A real laugh. The kind that made him believe in all possibilities—even those in dreams.

She didn't answer right away, but he could tell she was tempted to say yes. "I still don't know why you want to marry *me*."

He kissed her with all the passion she'd unleashed in his formerly barren soul, and when they were both breathless and laughing, he said, "Because with you, I'll be living my dream, Kat. Instead of just reading about the Old West, I get to move to the Black Hills, make mad, passionate love to the prettiest gal in the county—who also happens to be my wife—and raise bison in my spare time."

"What about being a stepdad to Jordie and Tag?"

"I'm looking forward to the challenge of convincing them I'm not a complete nerd."

"Good luck with that," she said, imitating her eldest son's disdain to a T.

Jack put both hands over his heart as if wounded and staggered backward. "As soon as I get to the Hills, we'll sit down and I'll tell you about my dad. He was a great guy who had got taken advantage of. I spent a lot of time thinking he was a chump, and I think I was so worried the same thing could happen to me that I missed out on a lot of life. He never would have wanted that for me, and I'm pretty sure he was behind my decision to walk into that bar in Deadwood that night."

"Why?"

"When I was a little kid, I called him Pop. I'd actually forgotten that. But when I looked at the name of the bar—Pop's—I remember thinking how ironic it was that my first stop on my walk on the wild side was a place that shared the name with a man who ruined his life by taking a foolish risk."

"What kind of risk?"

He shook his head. "Not an unreasonable one. He was just trying to please everybody while still honoring his own passion for helping people. I'd forgotten that, too. But now I know that somewhere in heaven my dad is smiling with all his might."

She looked thoughtful a moment, then asked, "What about your mom? I don't think she's going to be quite as pleased with all these changes you're proposing."

"One major hurdle at a time, okay? You have people in your life who will probably try to hold tight to the

status quo, too, but we'll deal with them in time. Together. If you say yes."

In time.

The phrase struck Kat as appropriate. She'd fallen in
love with him in another era. They'd had a crash course
of courting in two weeks. But the fact that she'd turned
to him without hesitation in her son's time of need
seemed a clear sign. He was the one.

But was she the right woman for him?

He stroked his thumb across her brow. "Listen, Kat,
I won't push you into my agenda. We have all the time
in the world—baby or no baby. But you need to know
one thing. I'm the most goal-oriented, single-minded
person you've ever met. That's the part I got from my
mother. I'm moving to Sentinel Pass. I've already
talked to a couple of builders in the area. I'm looking
into what I need to get licensed in the state and move
my business."

He paused to make his point. "But I don't intend to
be the workaholic my father was. I want to explore the
Hills with you and the boys every summer when you're
not teaching. I want us to be a family—just as soon as
you're ready."

Ready? She'd been ready her whole life for what he
was offering. If she was brave enough to take a giant
leap. Maybe she wasn't the best woman for him, but she
was the one he wanted…and she wanted him. She was
tired of doing this alone, being the matriarch of her
herd. She was ready to share the dream.

She glanced into the backyard. The boys looked relaxed and happy. Even serious Tag. They needed Jack,
too, she realized.

"Before I give you my answer to your proposal, I think you should know that I fell in love with Mad Jack first."

"Beg your pardon?"

"He was in my dream, too. That first night in Custer. I loved how he knew his own mind and didn't give a damn what other people thought of him. That didn't seem to fit the image I had of you back then. I'd just given you a temporary tattoo to impress your ex-fiancée, remember?"

His head bobbed. "Okay. I'll give you that. But what do you mean you fell in love with Mad Jack. He was in my dream."

"He was in mine, too. And I was Katherine. Strong, confident, a woman on a mission. I didn't think she was needy, like me."

He gave a soft snort. "You're the matriarch of your herd, Kat. Everything you've accomplished in your life, you've done alone. Just like Katherine."

"But she was loved—until her family died."

He pulled her close. "Oh, sweetheart, you were loved. Your family just had a lousy way of showing you. But your sons adore you. And I plan to spend the rest of my life proving just how much I love you." He kissed her tenderly, then asked one more time, "Will you marry me?"

She answered with all her heart, on behalf of the woman she was and the woman she knew she could be. "Yes."

CHAPTER EIGHTEEN

JACK HUNKERED DOWN over his horse's neck, trying to breathe air that wasn't filled with fine crystals of blowing snow. The storm had taken everyone by surprise. His friends had begged him to stay the night in town, but he didn't dare. He had too much to lose if something went wrong. He had to make sure Katherine was okay.

His horse knew the way and Jack trusted the animal's instincts. One hoof ahead of another and they finally made it to a clearing that looked vaguely familiar. A roofline. The faint scent of smoke.

He put the horse in the shelter of the barn and said a short prayer that he'd be able to find his way to the house—not sixty yards away. The barn door was yanked from his hand by the wind with a force that made his blood run cold. He squinted into the white wall of nothing.

He knew the general direction. He'd walked the same path every day for the past six months. But he'd heard stories of people frozen to death mere feet from their door. He lowered his chin, put his shoulder to the wind and took his first step. That was when he saw the rope tied to the hitching post.

He knew instantly who had put it there and why. Hand over hand, using the rope as a guide, he fought his way to the house. Without it, he might easily have wandered off course and died in a snowbank.

When he reached the porch, he stomped his boots and brushed off the thick, wet covering of ice and snow from his jacket. Despite the gloves he was wearing, his fingers felt numb. But his heart and mind were brightly alive with determination to make certain she was okay.

He opened the door and stepped inside. It took a moment for his eyes to adjust to the dim light from the fire in the hearth. Not the banked glow of embers one usually set at night but a well-tended cooking fire that held a kettle of bubbling water. A few feet away was the copper tub he'd bought her as a wedding present.

She was expecting him. Waiting. So in tune with him that not even the turbulent weather could keep her from sensing his intent to make it home—no matter what.

He looked around and spotted her. In her family's rocking chair she'd brought overland. She was watching his every move, but without missing a beat, she told the baby in her arms, "I told you your daddy was coming, little girl. No matter what, he'd get back to us, safe and sound."

Jack shrugged off his coat and hung it over the peg she'd asked him to install behind the door. A small triumph of civilization, she'd claimed. Her nod of approval went straight to his heart. He'd spent every day since they met trying to earn her respect in every way that counted.

In two strides he crossed the room and went down on one knee beside the rocking chair. He blew on his hands to warm them, then touched the schoolmarm's face. "Hello, wife."

Their kiss was tender, but it sparkled with the heat and desire they'd both found had grown in their union. He touched his baby girl's hand. The child's delicate little fingers wrapped around his.

He started to pick her up, but looked down a moment and thought better of it. "Maybe I better remove this first," he told his wife. "Don't want our darling Daisy to get scratched."

With a twist and a tug, his hand came away with a shiny star-shaped badge nestled in his palm. The gunslinger had gone legit. Love had changed him.

Jack looked at Katherine, the schoolmarm. So beautiful. So strong and compassionate and forgiving. So…Kat. She rocked forward and kissed him. "I love you, Jack."

THE WORDS ECHOED outside his dream and Jack opened his eyes. The woman of his dream was there, just inches away from him. Eyes wide. A knowing smile on her lips.

He blinked, trying to recall the images that had felt so very real. "I was dreaming. A snowstorm. We had a baby. I mean, Mad Jack and Katherine had a baby." If he closed his eyes, Jack could almost smell his child's scent. "I don't know what I mean."

Kat snuggled close, her head fitting just under his chin. "We'll have our own someday, Jack. You heard what the doctor said. Stress. That's why my body was so screwed up. But you're here now, and everything is going to be okay."

He knew that. He did. But there was still a lot to do. And even though it was still considered summer, winter would arrive before they knew it. His dream reminded him of that. He kissed her long and hard, then scooted out of bed. "I have to meet the pool crew at the house this morning. The solar-heating unit arrived yesterday. So much to do if we want to get you and the boys moved in before Christmas."

She groaned, but he knew she understood. Sitting up, she watched him dress. "I think they're happy about us, don't you agree? Really happy."

He looked around for his work boots but could only find one. "Who? The boys?"

She shook her head. "No. I mean, Mad Jack and Katherine. If we have a girl, can we name her Daisy? It's old-fashioned but sweet."

He stopped dead in his tracks. "You were there just now?"

Kat nodded. "I never doubted for a minute that you'd find your way home to us."

Jack believed her. He couldn't explain it, didn't even want to try, but he no longer questioned their subliminal connection.

She stretched. In the two weeks since Jordie's accident and their subsequent return to the Hills, she'd made peace with the fact that she wasn't pregnant. She actually seemed happy that she had a choice about whether she wanted Jack in her life.

Thankfully, she'd decided that everything happened for a reason—and the reason was love. She loved him and wanted to marry him as soon as they had time.

"By the way, the first piece of furniture we buy for our newly remodeled home has to be a rocking chair," she said. "I want one just like Libby's. The next time we have a book club there, you'll have to check it out."

Jack had been staying in Hill City while he supervised the remodeling of his newly purchased home. He spent every night that the boys were with their fathers in Kat's bed. Where they used protection. This time, Kat said, they were going to do things right.

That was fine with Jack as long as they sealed the deal soon. He was pushing for a Christmas wedding, but Kat wanted to make sure she didn't spread herself too thin by student-teaching and planning a wedding. Jack was hoping to convince his sister to move to Sentinel Pass—even temporarily—to help him set up his new office and help Kat plan a wedding. Rachel had learned a few days earlier that her job had fallen victim to the downturn in the economy.

Jack looked around once more, but still didn't see his boot. With a sigh, he started toward the door. "Maybe I left the other one on the deck," he muttered.

He'd only taken a couple of steps when he felt a sharp prick on the sole of his foot. "Youch!" he exclaimed.

Hopping around until he spotted something shiny partially buried in the old loop carpet, he reached down and picked it up. A cheap tin star. The kind a kid might wear while playing an Old West sheriff.

But it looked a little bit like the one… No. He shook his head and handed it to Kat. "Jordie's?" he asked.

Her eyes were big as she looked it over, front and back. "Umm...sure. If you say so. Who else could it belong to?"

Their gazes met, and even though they both did their best not to smile, within seconds Jack was back in bed with the woman he loved, rolling with mirth, laughing their heads off.

Who, indeed?

* * * * *

Be sure to catch the next installment in
Debra Salonen's
SPOTLIGHT ON SENTINEL PASS
miniseries!
Coming in May 2009
from Harlequin Superromance.

Celebrate 60 years of pure reading pleasure with
Harlequin® Books!

Harlequin Romance® is celebrating
by showering you with DIAMOND BRIDES
in February 2009.
Six stories that promise to bring a
touch of sparkle to your life, with
diamond proposals and dazzling weddings,
sparkling brides and gorgeous grooms!

Enjoy a sneak peek at Caroline Anderson's
TWO LITTLE MIRACLES,
available February 2009
from Harlequin Romance®

'I'VE FOUND HER.'

Max froze.

It was what he'd been waiting for since June, but now—now he was almost afraid to voice the question. His heart stalling, he leaned slowly back in his chair and scoured the investigator's face for clues. 'Where?' he asked, and his voice sounded rough and unused, like a rusty hinge.

'In Suffolk. She's living in a cottage.'

Living. His heart crashed back to life, and he sucked in a long, slow breath. All these months he'd feared—

'Is she well?'

'Yes, she's well.'

He had to force himself to ask the next question. 'Alone?'

The man paused. 'No. The cottage belongs to a man called John Blake. He's working away at the moment, but he comes and goes.'

God. He felt sick. So sick he hardly registered the next few words, but then gradually they sank in. 'She's got *what?*'

'Babies. Twin girls. They're eight months old.'

'Eight—?' he echoed under his breath. 'They must be his.'

He was thinking out loud, but the P.I. heard and corrected him.

'Apparently not. I gather they're hers. She's been there since mid-January last year, and they were born during the summer—June, the woman in the post office thought. She was more than helpful. I think there's been a certain amount of speculation about their relationship.'

He'd just bet there had. God, he was going to kill her. Or Blake. Maybe both of them.

'Of course, looking at the dates, she was presumably pregnant when she left you, so they could be yours, or she could have been having an affair with this Blake character before...'

He glared at the unfortunate P.I. 'Just stick to your job. I can do the math,' he snapped, swallowing the unpalatable possibility that she'd been unfaithful to him before she'd left. 'Where is she? I want the address.'

'It's all in here,' the man said, sliding a large envelope across the desk to him. 'With my invoice.'

'I'll get it seen to. Thank you.'

'If there's anything else you need, Mr Gallagher, any further information—'

'I'll be in touch.'

'The woman in the post office told me Blake was away at the moment, if that helps,' he added quietly, and opened the door.

Max stared down at the envelope, hardly daring to open it, but when the door clicked softly shut behind the P.I., he eased up the flap, tipped it and felt his breath jam in his throat as the photos spilled out over the desk.

Oh, lord, she looked gorgeous. Different, though. It took him a moment to recognise her, because she'd grown her hair, and it was tied back in a ponytail, making her look younger and somehow freer. The blond highlights were gone, and it was back to its natural soft golden-brown, with a little curl in the end of the ponytail that he wanted to thread his finger through and tug, just gently, to draw her back to him.

Crazy. She'd put on a little weight, but it suited her. She looked well and happy and beautiful, but oddly, considering how desperate he'd been for news of her for the past year—one year, three weeks and two days, to be exact—it wasn't only Julia who held his attention after the initial shock. It was the babies sitting side by side in a supermarket trolley. Two identical and absolutely beautiful little girls.

* * * * *

When Max Gallagher hires a P.I. to find his estranged wife, Julia, he discovers she's not alone— she has twin baby girls, and they might be his. Now workaholic Max has just two weeks to prove that he can be a wonderful husband and father to the family he wants to treasure.

Look for TWO LITTLE MIRACLES
by Caroline Anderson,
available February 2009
from Harlequin Romance®

CELEBRATE
60 YEARS
OF PURE READING PLEASURE
WITH HARLEQUIN®!

We'll be spotlighting a different series
every month throughout 2009
to celebrate our 60th anniversary.

Look for Harlequin® Romance in February!

Harlequin® Romance is celebrating by showering
you with Diamond Brides in February 2009.

Six stories that promise to bring a touch of sparkle to
your life, with diamond proposals and dazzling weddings,
sparkling brides and gorgeous grooms!

Collect all six books in February 2009,
featuring *Two Little Miracles* by Caroline Anderson.

*Look for the Diamond Brides miniseries
in February 2009!*

HARLEQUIN® *Romance*®

This February the Harlequin® Romance series
will feature six Diamond Brides stories featuring
diamond proposals and gorgeous grooms.

Share your dream wedding proposal and you could WIN!

The most romantic entry will win a diamond
necklace and will inspire a proposal in one of
our upcoming Diamond Grooms books in 2010.

In 100 words or less, tell us the most romantic
way that you dream of being proposed to.

For more information, and to enter
the Diamond Brides Proposal contest, please visit
www.DiamondBridesProposal.com

Or mail your entry to us at:

IN THE U.S.: 3010 Walden Ave., P.O. Box 9069, Buffalo, NY 14269-9069
IN CANADA: 225 Duncan Mill Road, Don Mills, ON M3B 3K9

REQUEST YOUR FREE BOOKS!
2 FREE NOVELS PLUS 2 FREE GIFTS!

HARLEQUIN®

Super Romance®

Exciting, emotional, unexpected!

YES! Please send me 2 FREE Harlequin Superromance® novels and my 2 FREE gifts (gifts are worth about $10). After receiving them, if I don't wish to receive any more books, I can return the shipping statement marked "cancel." If I don't cancel, I will receive 6 brand-new novels every month and be billed just $4.69 per book in the U.S. or $5.24 per book in Canada, plus 25¢ shipping and handling per book and applicable taxes, if any*. That's a savings of close to 15% off the cover price! I understand that accepting the 2 free books and gifts places me under no obligation to buy anything. I can always return a shipment and cancel at any time. Even if I never buy another book from Harlequin, the two free books and gifts are mine to keep forever.

135 HDN EEX7   336 HDN EEYK

Name	(PLEASE PRINT)	
Address		Apt. #
City	State/Prov.	Zip/Postal Code

Signature (if under 18, a parent or guardian must sign)

Mail to the **Harlequin Reader Service:**
IN U.S.A.: P.O. Box 1867, Buffalo, NY 14240-1867
IN CANADA: P.O. Box 609, Fort Erie, Ontario L2A 5X3

Not valid to current subscribers of Harlequin Superromance books.

Want to try two free books from another line?
Call 1-800-873-8635 or visit www.morefreebooks.com.

* Terms and prices subject to change without notice. N.Y. residents add applicable sales tax. Canadian residents will be charged applicable provincial taxes and GST. Offer not valid in Quebec. This offer is limited to one order per household. All orders subject to approval. Credit or debit balances in a customer's account(s) may be offset by any other outstanding balance owed by or to the customer. Please allow 4 to 6 weeks for delivery. Offer available while quantities last.

Your Privacy: Harlequin is committed to protecting your privacy. Our Privacy Policy is available online at www.eHarlequin.com or upon request from the Reader Service. From time to time we make our lists of customers available to reputable third parties who may have a product or service of interest to you. If you would prefer we not share your name and address, please check here. ☐

HSR08R

You're invited to join our Tell Harlequin Reader Panel!

By joining our new reader panel you will:

- Receive Harlequin® books—they are FREE and yours to keep with no obligation to purchase anything!
- Participate in fun online surveys
- Exchange opinions and ideas with women just like you
- Have a say in our new book ideas and help us publish the best in women's fiction

In addition, you will have a chance to win great prizes and receive special gifts! See Web site for details. Some conditions apply. Space is limited.

To join, visit us at
www.TellHarlequin.com.

COMING NEXT MONTH

#1542 THE STORY BETWEEN THEM • Molly O'Keefe
Jennifer Stern has left journalism to focus on life with her son. Then
Ian Greer—son of a former president—picks her to tell the true story of
his family, and it's a scoop she can't resist. But could her attraction to Ian
jeopardize the piece?

#1543 A COWBOY'S REDEMPTION • Jeannie Watt
Home on the Ranch
Kira Jennings just wants access across Jason Ross's land so she can subdivide
her property and sell it off…and save face with her CEO, aka grandfather.
Sure, there's bad blood between Jason and her brother. She didn't realize
exactly *how* bad. Until now.

#1544 THE HERO'S SIN • Darlene Gardner
Return to Indigo Springs
Good thing Sarah Brenneman doesn't judge a book by its cover. Otherwise she'd
believe what the town's gossips say about Michael Donahue. Instead, she's
impressed by his heroics. Still, can she believe what her heart is telling her
about Michael, or could those rumors end their romance before it even begins?

#1545 A KID TO THE RESCUE • Susan Gable
Suddenly a Parent
Shannon Vanderhoff knows that everybody and everything are temporary
gifts. So when she becomes guardian of her six-year-old, traumatized nephew,
how can she give him the help he needs without falling for him? It takes
Greg Hawkins's art therapy class to turn the child around…and it takes a kid
to create this loving family.

#1546 THE THINGS WE DO FOR LOVE • Margot Early
The man Mary Anne Drew loves is marrying someone else. So she buys a love
potion to win him back. Too bad the wrong man drinks it! Graham Corbett has
never shown any interest in Mary Anne before. Could the potion really work?
Or was she looking for love in the wrong place all along?

#1547 WHAT FAMILY MEANS • Geri Krotow
Everlasting Love
Debra and Will Bradley wanted their kids to know that family means
everything. Through hard and joyous times, Debra and Will have never
questioned that. Now Angie, their daughter, is pregnant—and separated.
Award-winning author Geri Krotow tells a memorable story of how marriage
and family define our lives.

HSRCNMBPA0109